FI
GOSPEL

Michel Faber is an internationally bestselling and award-winning author. His acclaimed novels include *Under the Skin*, *The Crimson Petal and the White* and *The Book of Strange New Things*, which was shortlisted for the Arthur C. Clarke Award and won the Saltire Book of the Year Award 2015. Born in Holland, brought up in Australia, he now lives in the UK.

'I was completely enthralled . . . Brilliantly wicked fun, but much more than that too . . . I read this in one sitting and will undoubtedly visit it again'
Sunday Herald Books of the Year

'Faber's dry, mischievous humour, and the grimly funny repercussions of Griepenkerl's hubris, stop this tale from ever becoming hard work . . . Hilariously entertaining'
Sunday Telegraph

'What he did for the Victorian novel in *The Crimson Petal and the White* . . . Faber now does for the bestselling books du jour'
Guardian

'Deliciously dark and witty, even hilarious'
Scotsman

'Burns with themes of faith and forgiveness'
Daily Telegraph

Also by Michel Faber

The FIRE GOSPEL

MICHEL FABER

CANONGATE

This paperback edition published in 2009 by Canongate Books

First published in Great Britain in 2008 by
Canongate Books Ltd, 14 High Street,
Edinburgh EH1 1TE

canongate.co.uk

2

British Library Cataloguing-in-Publication Data
A catalogue record for this book is available
on request from the British Library

ISBN 978 1 84767 279 7

Typeset by Palimpsest Book Production Ltd,
Falkirk, Stirlingshire

Printed and bound in Great Britain by Clays Ltd, Elcograf S.p.A.

Myths are universal and timeless stories that reflect and shape our lives — they explore our desires, our fears, our longings, and provide narratives that remind us what it means to be human. The Myths series brings together some of the world's finest writers, each of whom has retold a myth in a contemporary and memorable way. Authors in the series include: Alai, Karen Armstrong, Margaret Atwood, AS Byatt, Michel Faber, David Grossman, Milton Hatoum, Natsuo Kirino, Philip Pullman, Alexander McCall Smith, Klas Östergren, Victor Pelevin, Ali Smith, Su Tong, Dubravka Ugresic, Salley Vickers and Jeanette Winterson.

Thanks to Eva, always.

For I testify unto every man that
heareth the words of the prophecy of this book,
If any man shall add unto these things,
God shall add unto him the plagues
that are written in this book.

John, aka Iohannes, 'of Patmos', i.e. of unknown origin but resident on Patmos at time of writing, circa 95 or 96 AD, or possibly 68 or 69 AD, or possibly some other time, from an unnamed document later known as The Apocalypse, aka Revelation, reprinted in The Bible (1611), translated purportedly by Thomas Ravis, George Abbot, Richard Eedes, Giles Tomson, Sir Henry Savile, John Peryn, Ralph Ravens and John Harmar, but substantially based on The Bible (1526) translated by William Tyndale [uncredited].

Genesis

The museum curator swung open another antique door and, as if on cue, a lion's head fell off its body. A big stone lion's head, carved centuries ago: smack on the floor. Splinters of ceramic tile jumped up from the impact. The head rolled over and came to rest near the left paw, open-mouthed, front fangs smashed off, angry eyes staring up past the stump of its own neck to the ornate ceiling above.

'Unbelievable,' said Theo, feeling that some expression of awe was called for.

'No, not so unbelievable,' said the museum curator, glumly. 'The looters tried also to take that lion's head. They tried for a long time, with axes, crowbars, even guns. One of them shot the lion's neck and received a wound in the leg from the bouncing bullet. His friends only laughed. Then they moved on to the next thing.'

Theo walked into the denuded chamber, eyes lowered to the floor, as though he was humbled by the mighty sorrow of Allah in this desecrated sanctum, or at least admiring the exquisite ornamental tiles. In truth, he was on the lookout for traces of blood. There had been killing in this room, as well as the mishap with the looters' ricochet. But the place had been swept and mopped since then. Not very fastidiously, but enough. Here and there, a tiny glint of broken glass, a crumb of pottery, a wisp of fabric.

The curator, too, had been injured in the fracas. He had an untidy white bandage wrapped around his head, like a nappy, with a pinkish blush of imperfectly contained blood in the centre. It was a ridiculous mismatch with his dark-grey double-breasted suit, rich brown skin and expensive shoes. Why sport such a World War One napkin, when he could surely have got himself patched up with a few stitches and discreet Steri-Strips?

Making an exhibition of himself, Theo thought — knowing he was being outrageously unsympathetic.

This guy was a bona fide victim, no doubt about that. But there was a fine line between victims of tragic circumstance and born losers. Born losers were irritating as hell: shuffling around with their hang-dog expressions and untidy bandages. They attracted trouble and it didn't matter whether there was a war on or not, they would end up with their halo of undeserved suffering. Theo suspected that the curator was one of these characters. The grand injustice of war and the bloodied bandage on his head had accorded him the status of martyr and he was playing his role as best he could. The melancholy fatalism that newspaper journalists liked to describe as 'quiet dignity' radiated from him with every word and gesture.

I didn't trash your fucking country, thought Theo, and was ashamed of thinking it, but it was true. He was a linguist and research fellow from the Toronto Institute of Classical Studies, not some redneck Yankee soldier. In any case, it had been Iraqis who looted this museum, not Americans.

'Here we had manuscripts from the Ottoman empire,' said the curator, in a dolorous, soft-spoken monotone. 'We had scrolls from the Abbasid dynasty. We had an edition of the Qur'an, from 1787, inscribed by Catherine the Great.'

'Terribly sad,' said Theo.

'We had a clay tablet from Uruk, one of the most important cities in Mesopotamia, with a text in cuneiform that was not even yet deciphered.'

'Tragic,' said Theo. *Please don't tell me how important Uruk was; I'm not stupid*, he thought. And why did the curator insist on speaking English, anyway, when Theo had greeted him in perfectly good Arabic on the phone? It was as if the guy wanted to emphasise his humiliation in the face of the post-invasion catastrophe.

'We had wedding contracts from the seventh century BC,' lamented the curator, raising his head, so that the bandage rumpled up against his collar. 'From the time of Sennacherib.'

'Awful,' said Theo. He had an uneasy feeling that if he didn't take charge of the conversation soon, the curator would be compelled to remind him that Iraq was the cradle of civilisation, that it had once been a peaceful melting pot of learning and tolerance when most other nations were still in their brutish infancy, blah blah blah. All of which was true, but Theo was in no mood to hear it coming from the doleful little man with the nappy on his head. 'But listen, Mr Muhibb, if it doesn't sound too . . . ah . . . *brusque*, maybe we should focus on what's still here. I mean, that's why *I'm* here, after all.'

'They took everything, everything,' bewailed the curator, wringing his hands. 'There is nothing here remaining that a looter would deem worth to carry away.'

Theo sighed. He was accustomed to these protestations. They were like talismanic chants for the benefit of any eavesdroppers who might be planning additional raids. In order for a visitor to find out what treasures had been saved, what exhibits had been squirrelled away in a basement somewhere, or stashed pre-emptively in the museum staff's own homes, it was necessary to win the curator's trust, which would require hours of conversation and dinner and wine, and then the truth would emerge, artefact by artefact, and finally Theo could re-state the Institute's generous offer. Theo didn't know if he had the patience to go through with the rigma-role. For a start, he was trying to slim down, and a big, multi-course Arabic dinner would undo his efforts to lose his gut. Also, his inclination to forge convivial bonds with his fellow men was not exactly fervent at this juncture. His girlfriend had just told him, forty-five minutes ago, by mobile phone, that she needed some space to sort out her priorities. Her chief priority, he suspected, was a ruggedly handsome wildlife photographer called Robert.

'I'll be back in Toronto on Friday,' he'd said, broiling in the Mosul traffic on the way to the museum.

'I need some space *now*,' she'd said.

'Well, uh . . . I don't understand how I'm preventing you from getting it,' he'd said. 'I mean, I'm here, and you're there, alone. At least, I *think* you're—'

'I need you to understand that when you get back, things may not be the same.'

'Things?'

'Us.'

'So . . . why the suspense? Why not tell me now?' *Go on*, he'd thought. *Tell me you don't want an overweight academic when you can have a musclebound photographer who stalks fucking antelopes.*

'I have nothing to tell you. I just need some space, that's all.'

'Well . . . uh . . .' (he'd sneezed, an allergic reaction to the diesel exhaust polluting the humid air) 'be my fucking guest.'

Now, following the curator through the looted museum, Theo had an urge to grab him by the lapels of his suit and shout into his face. *Do you want the money or don't you? It's very simple. We display your treasures in our Institute for five years, in exchange for a nice big restoration package. At the end of the five years, Iraq is peaceful again, you've got a repaired museum, and you get your stuff back. Deal or no deal?*

'Excuse me,' said the curator, and motioned for them to stand still and listen. Faintly, a knocking could be heard from the front end of the building. (The doorbell had ceased to function; the PA system had been ripped out of the walls, leaving wires dangling down from the top corners of each room.)

'Excuse me,' repeated the curator. 'Please wait here a moment.' And he hurried to answer the summons.

Theo sat down on a polished wooden cabinet which had been toppled on its side and gutted of its drawers and index cards. He looked around the room; it was empty except for the jagged remains of a glass display case, a few wood shavings, and, in the far corner, an impossibly heavy Assyrian winged bull whose pedestal smelled of piss and disinfectant. He heard the museum's massive outside door opening and shutting. He wished he could light up a cigarette while he waited. It seemed absurd that in a place which had recently been gutted by thieves and yahoos, he should feel constrained not to befoul the air with a puff of tobacco smoke.

Suddenly, all the windows in the building exploded. There were three or four tremendous bangs, the first of which buffeted him like a hurricane gust. An impression of fierce heat and light came through from the outside world. Theo blinked. His spectacles had saved him from being blinded. His lap was sprinkled with tiny fragments of broken glass; they fell out of his hair when he looked down.

He stood up, and had the presence of mind to resist the urge to dust himself off with his naked palms. He tried to shake like a dog. Discovered that he was shaking already.

He moved towards the exit, then thought better of it. There were shouts out there, and more loud bangs. The curator and his absurd bandage were probably splattered all over the street, plastered to the walls and vehicles like upflung mud or fresh graffiti. Theo wished he'd been a little warmer to him, not quite so guarded. It seemed sinful to have considered somebody a pain in the ass two minutes before they got killed. But that was the trouble: in a fucked-up country, you could never predict which people would live forever to annoy the hell out of you and which ones were, in fact, giving you some of their last precious minutes on earth. And in a fucked-up country, it is simply not feasible to be generous to everyone. You end up dead yourself, or eaten alive by human parasites.

The sound outside was definitely gunfire. Iraq, at this moment in history, was full of excitable people who did not know or care where Toronto was on the world map, and who, if faced unexpectedly with a young Canadian male, might have difficulty imagining what to do with him other than shoot him in the chest. Theo hurried to the stairs at the centre of the building. There were, he recalled, toilets in the basement. He would hide in the toilets, or maybe in a storeroom, until everything was quiet.

He was halfway down the spiral stairs when he noticed that a wall-mounted, heavily pregnant bas-relief goddess he'd admired on his first trip down had been damaged in the blasts. Her belly – unexpectedly hollow – had been cracked open like an egg. He looked down at the floor of the basement where the shards of stone had fallen.

In amongst the shards, loosely swaddled in cloth, lay nine scrolls of papyrus.

Exodus

'The 25 *Cool Jazz Classics* CD is yours, I think,' she said.

He looked at her across the cardboard box of possessions he was holding to his chest.

'No, it's yours,' he said.

'I've never even heard it. Not once.'

'I don't dispute that,' he said. They were standing in the hallway of the flat they'd shared for four years and eight months. The bookcase, now that his books had been removed from it, was very sparsely stocked indeed: long stretches of creamy blank pine with the odd self-help paperback snoozing in a corner. 'But still it's not my CD. I bought it for you.'

'Right: *you* bought it, not me.'

'It was a Christmas gift,' he said, keeping his voice level. 'I thought it might lead you to an appreciation of jazz, if I started you off on the soft stuff that most people can get into.'

'I don't need "soft stuff",' she said. 'Or condescension.'

He put the box down at his feet, returned to the much-depleted CD cabinet, where her choice of music stared up at him with all its corporate rock insouciance. There were empty spaces next to her Bryan Adams and REO Speedwagon where his John Adams and Steve Reich had been; it was hard to believe they could have nestled side by side for half a decade without some sort of combustion. Theo removed 25 *Cool Jazz Classics* from the alphabetical arrangement he'd maintained since he and Meredith first moved in together. (V for 'various', rather than J for 'jazz': he recalled his hesitation over that decision as intimately as he recalled making love to her for the first time.) The CD was still sealed in Cellophane.

'You haven't even asked me how I got all these cuts on my face,' he said.

'Shaving?' she said.

'They're on my nose and forehead, too. Some of them should probably have had stitches.'

She sighed indulgently. 'OK, so tell me.'

'I was in a museum in Mosul when a bomb went off in the street outside. All the windows got blown in. I was showered with broken glass.'

She took a sip from the coffee mug she was holding. Her small wrist was white and her grip was too intense.

'We shouldn't be in Iraq,' she said.

'Well, yes, that's the considered opinion of many folks,' he remarked wryly. 'Including the people who blew up the politician's limousine, right outside the museum where I was. I heard on the news later that the politician's wife got . . . ah . . . distributed in lots of different directions. They found her head in the museum's reception area. It smashed through the window like a cannonball and bounced off the wall.'

Meredith was unimpressed by his little display of sublimated joy in the dismemberment of a female.

'I mean we shouldn't be there at all, none of us, for any reason,' she said. 'Not to fight, not to fix things up, not to offer money, not to talk, not to build, not to get oil, not to do news reports or make documentaries. We should just leave them to it. They were a hopeless rotten bunch of crazy people before we got there and we've made them more hopeless and rotten and crazy, and we should just get the hell out and let them do whatever they're gonna do and not even look at them again for a hundred years.'

She'd made herself breathless with her speech. There were tears in her eyes. He knew that depending on how he handled things from this moment on, she could be ten minutes away from a spectacular tantrum which would leave her shaken and craving the comfort of sex. He considered sticking around. But ten minutes seemed a long time.

'I'll carry these down to the car,' he said.

'Your girlfriend do that to you?' said Lowell when they'd started driving.

'Do what to me?'

Lowell was an old pal of Theo's from university days. Friendly enough to be called upon to help shift his stuff to the bachelor flat, not so friendly that the deal was emotionally complicated.

'The scratches on your face,' said Lowell.

'No, they're from broken glass.'

'Right.'

'I was in Iraq a few days ago, in a place called Mosul. I was visiting a museum. A bomb went off outside. It was an assassination. The building sustained some damage. So did I.'

Lowell laughed. 'Well, if you're gonna go on holiday in a war zone . . .'

'It wasn't a holiday. I was representing the Institute. I was hoping to arrange for some arte-facts to be shipped over here.'

'Bummer.'

'Yes, especially for the Iraqis that got killed in the attack.'

'Ah, they're used to it. And they go straight to Heaven, right? Or Paradise or Nirvana or whatever they call it. I read about that. Fifty hot virgins for every guy. It sure beats the hell out of clouds and harps.'

Theo smiled bemusedly. It was obvious that Lowell was not the right person with whom to share his great discovery.

On the back seat of the car, in amongst the books and CDs and clothing and shoes and the not-quite-functioning Walkman he thought he'd thrown out ages ago and the video camera and the bicycle helmet and the stoneware mug with the *Far Side* cartoon on it, lay a briefcase containing the nine scrolls. He was transporting them, at long last, on the final leg of their journey. Just a few more miles, from one Toronto suburb to another, and they would come to rest in their new home.

He could barely wait. Those papyri were burning a hole in his briefcase. They were like a stash of pornography that he'd been forced to delay getting to grips with. Not that there was anything kinky in his attraction to the scrolls; the porn comparison was just . . . a metaphor. A metaphor for the promises the papyri were urgently whispering from the back seat, of what they were going to do for him.

The scrolls were unquestionably authentic, in the sense that it was beyond doubt that they'd been sealed inside the bas-relief at the historical juncture when the sculpture was made, which was almost two thousand years ago. The airtight seal, combined with a preservative agent in the swaddling cloth, had kept the papyrus in superb condition: supple, robust, wholly spared the pulverous fragility that commonly afflicted ancient documents. This alone made the scrolls very, very special. Usually – not that the word 'usually' could be applied to the discovery of 2000-year-old scrolls, but let that pass – a find like this would cause a brief sensation in the newspapers, and then you wouldn't hear another word about it for years while a team of conservators and scientists debated the best way of extracting some vestiges of meaning from the pathetic mulch before it suffered its final collapse into decay. To find a scroll of this vintage that could simply be unrolled and read like the latest issue of the *Toronto Star* was unheard of.

To find nine of them, written in painstakingly clear script by a first-century Christian convert called Malchus, was miraculous.

*B*rothers and sisters, I thank you for your letters, and beg you to forgive me for waiting so long to answer them. I am unworthy of such patience. That is to say, the man called Malchus is unworthy, the man called Malchus deserves no more attention than a dead dog in the street; listen to him only insofar as his words can bear witness to the greatness of Jesus the Nazorean, the Messiah, the Son of God.

Prose-wise, it was not the most scintillating opening salvo, especially for an atheist like Theo. But what had electrified him in the Mosul museum when he'd first examined the scrolls was that they were written in Aramaic. Had they been written in Coptic Egyptian or Kurdish or Persian, or even in Classical Arabic (a language he could read passably well with the aid of Koranic glossaries), he would have felt that they were national treasures that manifestly did not belong to him. To remove them, even from a looted museum with burning vehicles and roasted human flesh all around it, would have been theft. But Aramaic . . . Aramaic was his baby. He knew it better than just about anyone in North America, better than many scholars in the eastern world. The coincidence of finding an Aramaic memoir — to have it literally falling at his feet — at a highly dramatic moment in his life, was too astounding to ignore. These scrolls were meant for him. There was no other explanation for it.

In truth, my life for the most part has been a worthless one, insofar as the life of any man before he becomes acquainted with Jesus the Messiah adds nothing of value to the world. My first thirty-five years, in my own conception during the living of them, were full of sweet achievements and bitter disappointments; but I see now that I contended against nothing and won nothing.

Since leaving the house of my mother, I have earned my bread in the following ways: as a scribe of the unimportant utterances of unimportant men who puffed themselves up to be great leaders, and as a gossip and informer. My official titles were not so. But these are the true words for my usefulnesses.

My first employment was in the court of procurator Valerius Gratus. My head was like a lantern, burning with the pride of serving a person of such high office. I translated his most trivial pronouncements from Roman into the popular tongue. For his more significant pronouncements, he had other scribes. Three years I did this. I might as well have bent my quill to a flow of ordure in the street, and written upon its surface as it sped along the gutter. But my hunger for advancement was very keen.

That was about as much as Theo had managed to read so far, what with the other things going on in his life. Apart from a few hours in planes, leafing through crumpled in-flight magazines and watching the uniformed handmaidens do their symbolic safety dances, he'd had no time to reflect. Getting from the museum to Baghdad Airport had been an experience and a half, filled with the sort of high-octane anxiety that seemed to be Iraq's principal domestic product. All sorts of things had happened to him – or *almost* happened to him – which, if Meredith had still been his girlfriend, would no doubt have impressed her mightily to hear about. And the fact that his various narrow scrapes were routine ones – just the run-of-the-mill dangers affecting anyone foolhardy enough to be in Iraq right now, rather than the specialised hazards associated with soldiering – gave them an added frisson of exoticism. He could've recounted them nonchalantly, in a low-key, good-humoured tone, similar perhaps to the tone used by a wildlife photographer describing close encounters with wild animals.

Anyway, enough of Meredith. He had the scrolls now, which were potentially a much bigger deal in his life than any female. Relationships, he could have anytime. Life-changing discoveries were not so easy to come by.

A higher agency wanted him to have them, that much was clear. At Baghdad Airport, with sweat pouring from his armpits, he'd handed in his suitcase at the check-in desk, having decided against putting the scrolls in his hand luggage. It was torture to surrender the suitcase onto a conveyor belt to possible oblivion, but he judged it was a lesser risk than trying to keep the papyri on his person while passing through security. He had no idea whether checked-in luggage was screened for suspicious objects; he kind of wished that it was, because of the sheer idiocy of making people stand in line while their handbags were X-rayed and tubes of toothpaste were confiscated. Why humiliate an old lady for having a nail file in her mouldy little purse when there was nothing to stop a terrorist stowing a suitcase filled with explosives in the hold of the plane? But OK, whatever. His suitcase had gone through.

In Athens, the fifteen minutes he spent waiting for his luggage to appear on the carousel caused him almost as much stress as his dash through the burning streets of Mosul. But again, a higher agency was looking after him. The suitcase rolled out, undamaged, unbroached. He immediately checked in to his Toronto flight, and, on arrival there, suffered the same fifteen minutes of anxiety, peering into the dark aperture at Baggage Reclaim. Again, his suitcase trundled casually into view. A big bunch of sweaty shirts and pants and socks, a creased jacket, and, wrapped snugly inside those grubby clothes, the greatest archaeological find in centuries – he'd whisked them from a war zone, pulled them out of the flames (so to speak) and brought them home.

Home? Well, not quite, not without a struggle. Shortly after touchdown in Toronto, Theo was presented with the tricky challenge of moving out of his flat, finding new accommodation and not physically attacking his suddenly-ex-girlfriend. It was at times like these that Canada's policy of discouraging gun ownership among members of the public seemed eminently sensible.

'You gonna be all right?'

Lowell's voice jolted Theo out of his reverie.

'I'll be fine,' he said, slightly annoyed at this attempt of Lowell's to forge one of those delicate guy–guy moments.

'You got stuff to keep you busy?'

'Sure. A big translation project.'

'Uh-huh.' Lowell looked unconvinced. Maybe he thought Theo was lying, or maybe he felt that shutting oneself in a crappy little apartment dicking around with a dead language was an unwise pursuit for a man in Theo's situation. Maybe he felt that a newly cuckolded discard should be out on the town, drinking with his buddies and getting laid.

'I mean big in every way,' said Theo. 'I have a feeling a whole new phase of my life is about to begin.'

'That's the spirit,' chirped his pal.

Malchus

*B*rothers and sisters in the Messiah! I write these words in lowest wretchedness; I hope that you will read them in highest gladness. My belly is afflicted with constant pains, and food passes through me without giving nourishment. The gnawing in my guts allows me no sleep. Four months I have been like this. My flesh is yellow, my eyes are yellow, the hairs fall from my head, and my innards make noises when all else is quiet. I scratch at my skin like a dog. Praise the Lord! Were it not for this mission he has chosen me for, I would be long dead and in the grave, I am certain!

But enough of my body and its ailments. The body is but a chariot for our spirit to ride. It matters not that my own chariot is fit only for firewood, nor that the wheels grind and the axles *creak. My spirit is seated in it even yet. Praise the Lord!*

Brothers and sisters, I thank you for the questions you have asked me in your letters, concerning the correct behaviour for those who dwell in Jesus. I beg your forgiveness for the long delay you have endured in awaiting my answers. You must know that since losing my position in the temple of Caiaphas, I have had no fixed abode. I flit from house to house like a bird, or shall I say rather, a rat. I tell everyone that I live in the house of my father. This is true, inasmuch as I live in the house of our heavenly Father, or expect very soon to take up my residence there! But while I scurry upon the earth, I must make arrangements that are not so perfect.

Your letters are kept in store for me by my father, likewise named Malchus, and I fetch them into my own hands as often as I can. But, unlike our beloved Jesus and his heavenly father, Malchus and Malchus were never a harmonious pair. And we are even less so, now that I have lost my posi-

tion at the temple, and now that I have scarcely a mite in my purse, and now that my face is disfigured and my body befouls the air around it. Each time I return to his house, my father addresses whoever stands near, whether they be servants or passersby, and speaks in a loud voice, saying, Can this be my son? Is this my fate, to have such a son? And many other speeches of this kind. Only after this ceremony has been completed am I admitted across his threshold, and permitted to fetch the letters that you have sent to me, brothers and sisters. But enough of that. I will speak of it no more. Praise the Lord!

You asked me, dear Azubah, in your last letter, what should be done when a man who is not in Jesus wishes to love a woman who is in Jesus. I cannot recall, from my conversations with Thaddaeus and James, any statement made by our Saviour on this matter. According to Thaddaeus, Jesus said many times that no man shall enter the kingdom of Heaven but through him. But they, that is to say Thaddaeus and James, did not ask our Saviour until he was gone from us, whether this meant that all good men in all the world, who have never heard a word spoken of Jesus, much less met him, through no fault of their own, are barred from entering the kingdom. James was of the belief that this must be so; the words of Jesus were clear. Thaddaeus disagreed, urging us rather to study the Messiah's general disposition when he moved through the everyday world. He, that is to say Jesus, often praised the righteous poor, observing them discreetly, and making example of them in his teachings. Thaddaeus recalled that there was on a certain day in the temple a widow who put an offering of only two copper coins in the temple alms-box, while before her were rich persons giving much more. I am sure I have told you this story in a previous letter; my memory is not what it was since I have suffered this sickness. I discharge my responsibilities in between foul embarrassments from both ends of my body.

But, to return to the story of the widow. For Thaddaeus, there was a greater meaning in the tale, beyond her admirable sacrifice of coins she could not spare. He noticed that Jesus let the widow leave the temple. He did not speak to her, or instruct his disciples to follow her. She dwelled in perfect ignorance of him, and, much as he loved her, he allowed it. Thaddaeus took this as proof that the righteous who are ignorant of the Messiah are not damned. The damned are those who hear of the Messiah and scorn him. As further proof, he, that is to say Thaddaeus, pointed out that the Messiah will return in glory and judgement very soon, certainly within our lifetime. Yet in our lifetime, witness as hard as we may, we cannot hope to enlighten more than a few hundred persons. Does this mean that the kingdom of Heaven will be opened to a few hundred persons only, and closed to all the other thousands of persons in the world?

At this point, as I recall, Thaddaeus and James would begin to dispute with raised voices and robust gestures of hands.

My own belief is that the kingdom of Heaven will have many courts, and many gardens and gates and chambers, and that the ignorant righteous will dwell in some of these, while the truly saved will dwell with our Saviour in the inner temple. And I believe Thaddaeus to be correct, in saying that those who have heard the call of Jesus but rejected him, will be excluded. So, my counsel to you, dear Azubah, is that a woman who is in Jesus, and who is pursued by a lover who is not, has a heavy duty. For, while the man remains ignorant, he may yet enter the kingdom, whereas if he hears your witness of the Messiah, and laughs in your face, he will be damned. So your persuasion must be powerful indeed, or you will succeed only in robbing him of his life hereafter.

However, furthermore, I understand that many weeks have elapsed since you sent me your letter. Life demands action, and actions follow swiftly upon provocation. In the case of the woman and the man, I imagine that whatever was not yet done when you wrote your letter is since done, and cannot be undone, and I have spilled ink for no purpose. But, even so, you asked a question and I answered it. Praise the Lord!

This guy is a bore, thought Theo. *A total fucking bore*.

It was 1 a.m. in his new apartment. He leaned back in his unfamiliar chair, bracing his knees against the bottom of the unfamiliar table, and stared at the computer screen where Malchus's words hung in translation. The original scroll was stretched out on his desktop, prevented from rolling itself up by four heavy coffee mugs. Empty mugs, obviously. It would be a shame if the scrolls, having survived immaculate for two thousand years, were rendered illegible by a coffee spill. Ideally, he would have them pressed between two sheets of hinged plexiglass, but equipment like that was only available at the Institute, and it was probably harder to smuggle a viewing case out of the Institute than to smuggle the scrolls out of Iraq.

Theo pinched the bridge of his nose, screwed his eyes tight. All things considered, he was a great deal less elated than he'd expected to be at this stage of proceedings. He was full of bad pizza, Pepsi and chocolate chip cookies. His head throbbed and his back ached. He missed his expensive ergonomically designed chair, which Meredith had somehow neglected to remind him was his, unlike the 25 *Cool Jazz Classics* CD. There was a bad taste in his mouth, not just from the so-called comfort food, but from the conversation he'd had earlier that day with his superiors at the university. They were unimpressed with his near-death experience in Iraq; all they cared about was that they'd paid to get him there and paid to get him back and there was nothing to show for it.

'For God's sake, the curator died!' Theo reminded them. 'Splattered all over the street!'

'You could have stayed a little longer,' said one of his superiors. 'In Mosul, I mean. Another curator would have been appointed. You could have dealt with him . . .'

'Or her,' added his other superior. 'It might have been a propitious juncture, actually. In the upheaval following this . . . ah . . . incident. The new curator might have been eager to appear decisive and competent.'

Theo couldn't believe what he was hearing. Meredith always complained that he was cold and calculating: she should get a load of these guys!

Custodians of civilisation! Hyenas circling a scene of carnage!

Good thing he hadn't told them about the scrolls. It was none of their business. As soon as he was financially secure, he would tell them where they could stick their precious Institute.

In his horrid new flat, Theo leaned back, and the cheap chair creaked dangerously. Soon enough, he would buy a high-quality chair just like the one Meredith had filched from him. He would buy whatever he wanted. Including some Alka-Seltzer. Actually, he wished he could buy the Alka-Seltzer right now, but the shops were shut. The medicine cabinet in the bathroom was empty except for a tiny bottle of nail polish remover, a token of his landlady's largesse. To top it all off, the walls in this flat were painted orange. Who paints walls orange, for God's sake? Japanese drug addicts? Semi-professional New Age masseuses? Elderly Dutch homosexuals? No wonder the rent was reduced. It had nothing to do with the busted microwave or the temperamental shower. It was the fucking orange walls.

He took a deep breath, counselled himself to relax. He lit up a smoke, turning his back to the scroll while igniting the cigarette's tip, just in case a stray spark might leap through the air and set fire to his future. He inhaled the menthol-flavoured drug, blew a cloud towards the orange walls, inhaled again, blew again. He smoked hurriedly, without pleasure, as though he were standing at a bus stop and had mere seconds to finish the thing off before the bus left without him. When he was finished, he extinguished the butt on a fragment of pizza and left it embedded in the mozzarella.

His treasured copy of John Coltrane's *Stellar Regions* was playing through the computer speakers, the aural equivalent of a dog marking freshly claimed territory with its scent. A home wasn't a home until Coltrane had sprayed it with his saxophone. Except that *Stellar Regions* was currently turned down to an almost inaudible volume, for fear of upsetting the neighbours, who'd introduced themselves yesterday afternoon bearing a gift of cookies. As if to say, *You wouldn't make life hell for people who've given you cookies, would you?* Trane's wild sax improvs blended with the whirring cooler fan of the PC, producing an ambient hybrid that was faintly irksome.

Theo considered going to bed. But then remembered that he'd spent one night in this apartment's bed already, and hadn't liked it. The bed creaked when you turned from side to side. There was no Meredith in it and its sheets were too new. The room was small and on the ceiling there was a small red light – mandatory for safety purposes – blinking on and off all night. The light was like an insect trapped in the room; you wanted to get up and slap it.

In this apartment, with its uncomfortable bed and alien lights and orange walls, it was difficult to hold on to the conviction that he would soon have enough money to buy any house he wished, anywhere. He must have faith. He mustn't forget that the scrolls were historical relics on a par with the pyramids. Yes! The pyramids! Right here on his desk, weighted down with coffee mugs, was a marvel of antiquity. The Colossus of Rhodes, the Temple of Artemis, the Hanging Gardens of Babylon: all of them destroyed and turned to myth, but the scrolls . . . the scrolls were here, and he possessed them.

And yet, until other people recognised their fabulous value, the scrolls were just part of the contents of his flat, along with the empty pizza box and the not-quite-functioning Walkman. That dazzling, euphoric moment of discovery, when he first glimpsed them on the floor of the Mosul museum, and his future was illuminated in a glow of anticipated glory, had dimmed now. Love at first sight can't last. He'd seen the scrolls, he'd taken them; now what? The challenge of converting them into a brilliant future was trickier than he'd thought.

Sure, millions of people would be interested in his discovery. But he couldn't sell the scrolls to millions of individuals. What he *could* sell was a translation of Malchus's words from Aramaic into English, and this was where self-doubt came in. And not just because Malchus's prose was dull beyond belief.

The very process of translating the scrolls demystified them, made them humdrum. As a professional linguist engaged on a task, Theo was subject to the usual niggly little worries, fretting about imperfect equivalents of Aramaic verb stems and the ethics of changing the syntax from Verb Subject Object to Subject Verb Object. In his head, he deconstructed the text into individual words and clauses, until the original grand edifice, an Eighth Wonder Of The World, was reduced to an inventory of stones. Then he reassembled those stones in digital typeface on a computer screen mounted on a plastic pedestal. The result looked no different from anything else in his PC, figments of the same universe as eBay and CNN.com and the offers of cheap Viagra and penis enlargement in his email inbox.

He looked across at the scroll, pinioned on his desk, and tried to remind himself that these inky marks on ancient paper were astonishing, sensational, priceless.

'I have spilled ink for no purpose,' was the first sentence his eyes lit upon.

Could that be true? No, it couldn't be, it mustn't be.

OK, so Malchus was a bore. So what? This guy was not your average fundamentalist gasbag from

Poopville, Missouri, writing an internet blog. He was the author of the oldest surviving piece of Christian literature! He knew two of Jesus's disciples personally! He was a full-time evangelist at a time when Saint Paul was still a government bullyboy called Saul of Tarsus, hauling illicit believers off to jail. Malchus might be a moaning nonentity, but he was Important with a capital fucking I!

Theo applied himself with fresh determination to the task at hand.

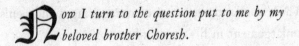

ow I turn to the question put to me by my beloved brother Choresh.

Theo chewed his lower lip. Translate 'Choresh' as 'George'? Jabbing at his keyboard's backspace bar he deleted seven letters, then typed 'George' in their place. Then he deleted 'George' and typed in 'Choresh'. The time displayed at the bottom right corner of his computer screen was 1:27. The cold bed was waiting for him, there was half a pound of salami-encrusted, Pepsi-marinated mozzarella lodged in his stomach, and Meredith probably had her legs wrapped round the neck of the wildlife photographer by now.

ou ask after the true name of Thaddaeus. Thaddaeus, when I enquired of him regarding this matter, told me that his name was Thaddaeus. Therefore I must pass on to you that his name is Thaddaeus.

'Fucking hell!' cried Theo in frustration, and went to bed.

Next morning, bleary-eyed, his glasses slightly fogged by hot coffee, Theo translated the lines that followed.

owever, speaking discreetly among trust-worthy friends, I think it would not be disloyal to say that if you asked this same question not of myself, but rather of Thaddaeus's mother, she would tell you that his name is Judas.

For by that name was he known, until the actions of the other Judas, that is to say the Betrayer, brought shame upon the name. Furthermore, in the event that you should ever meet Judas, that is to say Thaddaeus, in person, which you may likely have the good fortune to do, for he has embarked on a journey of devoted witnessing to the glory of our Saviour, I advise you to greet him as Thaddaeus, and on no account speak the other name. For it is a point of soreness with him.

Which I understand well enough. For I have known both Judases, and indeed I was present in the temple of Caiaphas when Judas the Betrayer was given his payment. And it is as galling for me, as it is for Thaddaeus, to observe how Judas has since grown fat and lazy upon that money.

But most grievous for me is the knowledge that I was standing by at the precise moment when the betrayal of our Saviour was arranged, and felt no disquiet of my own. I felt only a prick of envy at the size of the sum, which seemed to me overly generous for the service rendered.

MALCHUS

Such was the filthiness of my heart, in those last days of my old life, before I stood on Golgotha and my heart was scalded clean by the blood of our Saviour.

Such was Malchus.

Numbers

'Two hundred and fifty thousand dollars, take it or leave it,' said Baum, leaning back in his chair until the sunlight from the window behind him turned the lenses of his spectacles into opaque circles of brilliance. 'That's a quarter of a million.'

Theo frowned. The word 'million' hung in the air, a distracting illusion. The true figure, lacking that magical seventh digit, was merely in the thousands. Which was not what his research into author advances had led him to expect.

'The book could easily generate that much in the first few hours of publication,' he protested. 'I'd have to be completely stupid.'

'On the contrary,' said Baum, not in the least offended. 'If sales really do go through the roof, you're a big winner. You earn out your advance in a single afternoon, and then it's royalties forever after.'

'Yes, very tiny royalties,' said Theo, striving to sound wry rather than exasperated. 'Maybe the tiniest, longest-delayed royalties in any publishing contract, ever. I feel I need a refresher course in algebra just to understand how the micro-fractions would eventually add up to my first dollar. Any half-decent lawyer or agent would look at me and just shake their head.'

Baum swivelled forward once again, and fixed Theo with a kindly, merciless stare.

'But they've already done that, haven't they?' he wheezed. 'The half-decent ones and the decent ones and maybe the not-so-decent ones. Nobody wants to represent you.'

'That's not true,' said Theo. He felt himself blushing and when he blushed the scars on his face itched. They'd healed awkwardly; he really should have got them stitched, instead of rushing home to be humiliated by Meredith. He was damned if he would let himself be humiliated again. 'I only approached two agents,' he insisted, 'or five, if you count the three that didn't answer my calls. Of the agents I had meetings with, one ended up saying she doesn't handle anything religious in nature, which was annoying, because she could've told me that on the phone. The other seemed keen to go ahead. Very keen.'

'But you're here on your lonesome.'

'I . . . I just didn't like the guy. We didn't click. And so I decided to see what would happen if I approached a publisher myself. I mean, this book is fantastically important; it's not as if anyone is going to need convincing that people will want to read it.'

'Sure,' agreed Baum softly. 'Sure.' He removed his glasses and wiped them on his tie, gazing vaguely at his desk. He devoted a full thirty seconds to one lens, then began on the other. All the while, in other rooms of the office floor occupied by Elysium, telephones kept ringing and being answered by employees. Baum's own phone flashed intermittently but made no sound except for the occasional click, like a nervous person swallowing. Theo looked around the office, taking in the stacks of identical hardbacks next to the watercooler, the display case of past publications, the posters for Elysium's one and only bestseller, the African statuettes, the wall-mounted cover designs, the unopened cardboard boxes and, in a far corner, the mound of manuscripts (some still sealed in outsize Jiffy bags) which must be the Slush Pile. Theo hadn't expected the Slush Pile to be a literal pile. He'd assumed it would be something less pitiful and publicly on view.

'A book like yours', said Baum, 'gets tongues wagging in an industry like ours. I'm under no illusions. You approached Oxford University Press; Knopf; Harcourt; Grove Atlantic; Little, Brown; HarperCollins; Penguin . . . maybe others I didn't hear about. I suspect you approached just about every publisher that has a sizeable turnover. And then you came to me.'

'Elysium is a highly regarded publisher of academic texts,' said Theo.

'So it is, so it is,' said Baum breezily. 'It is also – or was, until two years ago – a small fish, an also-ran, a little sparrow hanging around the hyenas hoping that when the big orgy of feasting is over, there might be some overlooked morsel left to scrounge.' His voice was developing a harder edge. For the first time since ushering Theo into his office, he no longer resembled the mild-mannered proprietor of a second-hand bookstore. 'Then, two years ago, on one of those jamborees of slaughter that publishers call book fairs, when all the self-evidently big books had been dragged away in a trail of fresh blood and I was left with the offal and the fragments of toenail as usual, I came upon a manuscript by a Norwegian schoolteacher, translated by a not-*quite*-bilingual translator, of games that parents should play with their children in order to teach them arithmetic. That little book, as I'm sure you know, has become a surprise bestseller for Elysium. In fact, it has outperformed every other book from that book fair, all the hyped novels that were auctioned for astronomical sums, all the chauffeur-driven manuscripts, all the gold-plated proofs. It has stomped on them with its little knitted Scandinavian booties. And we are selling thousands of copies a week to worried parents who want to sing the multiplication tables with their kids at bedtime.'

Theo sat silent. When someone was springloaded, it was best to let them speak their piece.

'Do I sound like a man with a grudge, Theo? Very well, I am a man with a grudge. I've been a sparrow hanging around hyenas for too many years. I've grown old waiting for my chance. I know very well that my kiddie arithmetic book won't persuade any prestigious authors to give their next magnum opus to Elysium. *Sing Times Seven* will be a fluke, and at the next Frankfurt Book Fair, I will be mobbed by agents trying to sell me books about teaching your dog geometry via jazz ballet.'

'My book isn't about teaching dogs geometry,' Theo reminded him. 'For God's sake, Mr Baum, it's a new Gospel! It's a previously unknown account of the life and death of Jesus, written in Aramaic, the language Jesus himself spoke. In fact, it will be the *only* Gospel written in Aramaic: the others are in Greek. And it's earlier than Matthew, Mark, Luke and John, years earlier. I can't understand why publishers aren't falling over themselves to put it out – 99.99 per cent of books aren't important, not *really*. This one *is*.'

Baum smiled sadly. 'Theo, you keep calling it a book. That's obstacle number one. It isn't a book. It's thirty pages of text, max, if it were printed in quite a roomy font with generous margins. We cannot publish it as a pamphlet. So, the obvious solution is that we pad it out with your account of how you found the scrolls, how you got them back from Iraq, some fascinating facts about the history and structure of the Aramaic language, what you had for breakfast on the morning you arrived back in Toronto, and so on and so on and so on. That part is a risk for Elysium. Because we have not the faintest idea if you can write. Which, despite what you may have concluded from *Sing Times Seven*, is still an issue of concern for me.'

'I've written a number of articles on Aramaic for linguistics journals,' said Theo.

'And your payment for those articles, I have no hesitation in guessing, was a couple of free copies of those journals. Not 250,000 dollars.' Before Theo could object again, Baum went on: 'Obstacle number two: the scrolls, arguably, are stolen goods. This is why Oxford University Press and Penguin and all the others won't commit, and you know it.'

Theo was ready for this one. He'd prepared his

defence. 'I just can't see it that way; my conscience is clear. If you'd asked the museum whether they owned those scrolls before I came on the scene, they would've said, "What scrolls?" They *had* no scrolls, as far as they were concerned. I've studied the museum's inventory, every last statue and coin and tablet they owned before the war started. The scrolls weren't on it. So, officially, they don't exist. They might as well have fallen out of a tree in the street outside, or washed up on a beach.'

Baum nodded wearily. 'Either of those scenarios would have been a much safer bet, legally speaking, but it's too late to start spinning them now. The point is that it's a grey area. You took something the museum didn't know it had. Something extremely valuable that the Iraqi nation would surely wish to keep a hold of, in normal circumstances. Of course, there's a big question mark hanging over what they'll do if we publish. They may do nothing. They're kind of . . . preoccupied with other things, after all. The whole concept of an Iraqi nation, and who speaks for it, and who represents it, is up in the air. But I suspect that somebody in Iraq, sometime, surely will demand the scrolls be returned. Which isn't necessarily a problem for our book, which will've sold whatever it's going to sell by then. Or maybe it *is* a problem, if some Iraqi lawyer argues that our profits are illegal and we should forfeit them. I don't know. It's a grey area. I can well understand why other publishers are hesitant to go there. I may live to regret going there myself.'

'What about the Bible?' Theo was speaking a little too loudly now; he couldn't help it. 'Anybody can publish a Bible if they want to, can't they? Or a Dickens novel for that matter, a Mark Twain novel, *Gulliver's Travels*, anything that's older than a hundred years. OK, there may be some person or institution that owns the original manuscript, but that's a separate issue. The text, the actual words, are out of copyright. They're in the public domain.'

'Which brings us to obstacle number three,' said Baum. 'Our man Malchus has been dead a lot longer than Dickens. Which means that when our book comes out, the only parts of it that will have the cast-iron protection of copyright law will be *your* parts. Your thrill-packed account of your sweaty forehead when you thought your suitcase might get impounded by security at Baghdad Airport. Your description of how many Band-Aids you had to apply to your face. And so on. Copyright will keep every word of it sacred. Whereas Malchus's part will be all over the internet within forty-eight hours, or however long it takes somebody to type the text onto a website.'

'That's not true. My *translation* will be copyright.'

'Of course, of course. They'll have to paraphrase, change a few words here and there. Or maybe they won't bother. The internet is a slippery beast. Cut off one website, and another seven spring up in its place. I'm getting an ulcer just thinking about it. But I still want to publish. Is that dedication or what?' He smiled. His teeth were false. He was, as he claimed to be, an old man.

'The contract is still outrageous,' said Theo.

'The contract is not outrageous,' said Baum. 'The

contract gives you a quarter of a million dollars and it gives me half a million headaches. Please remember that Elysium is, or was, an academic publisher. In academic publishing, usually, very little money changes hands. Authors often don't even get an advance. We at Elysium are not in the business of bestsellers, we are in the business of . . . of . . .' Baum leapt up from his chair, crossed over to the nearest bookcase, and pulled out a handful of slim volumes. He whacked them down on the desk for Theo to examine, one, two, three, four, like playing cards. *Gothic Ascetic: The Paradoxical Oeuvre of Giovanni Piranesi* was one. *The Smallest Intimations of Tomorrow: Women Poets and Political Oppression in Iran, 1941–1988* was another.

'Yes, but my book is in a whole different class from these,' said Theo. 'I don't mean in terms of quality, I mean in terms of the sheer numbers of people who'll be interested. There's just no comparison. This book is going to explode.'

Baum wandered away from the desk, stood in front of a poster for *Sing Times Seven* on which two cartoon children in a sudsy bathtub were blowing numbers at their delighted parents. The mild, vaguely despondent expression had settled back onto Baum's face and he once again resembled an unworldly second-hand bookseller.

'Yes,' he murmured. 'I fear it will.'

Every Word That Proceedeth
Out Of The Mouth

The make-up girl dabbed at his forehead with a sable brush. She frisked his nose, stroked his eyebrows with the tip of her manicured finger. It was almost erotic, especially since she had a low-cut blouse and a lacy pink bra and she was leaning over him in his dressing-room chair.

'So, what's *your* book?' she enquired.

'It's called *The Fifth Gospel*,' he said. He had a childish desire to fetch it out of his bag and show her. Elysium had really gone to town on the cover design: a die-cut, two-fold jacket, the outer flap of which was a photographer's re-creation of Golgotha, with a crucifix shape cut out, affording a glimpse of the second cover beneath, a high-res reproduction of Malchus's handi-work. Despite Baum's protestations about being an academic publisher at heart, and despite the low-budget, unpretentious cover of *Sing Times Seven*, Elysium had clearly evolved with great speed into the major league. Even the title was embossed in silver foil.

'Is it gonna be a movie?' said the make-up girl.

'No,' he said. (Although . . . who could predict the ways of Hollywood?) 'It's not fiction, it's real. I discovered some scrolls, ancient scrolls written in the first century by a man called Malchus. He met Jesus. Actually met him.'

'Wow,' said the girl. She didn't sound too over-whelmed.

'You know the other four Gospels, the ones in the Bible? Matthew, Mark, Luke and John?'

'Sure,' she said, her eyes half shut as she powdered his chin.

'Two of those guys definitely never met Jesus, and the other two did, but we can't be sure if they were really kosher, if you'll excuse the expression.'

'Do I look Jewish?' she asked, a wrinkle spoiling the pellucid patina of her brow.

'No. I meant that we don't know if the Gospels of Matthew and John were originally by Matthew and

John. The earliest surviving manuscripts were written a long time after the events, by people who must've been copying copies of copies. Copies of what? We don't know. Maybe Matthew and John did write their memoirs. Maybe someone else did, fifty years later.'

As he babbled, he had the uneasy feeling he might be blowing his load prematurely, here in a backstage make-up chair, instead of in front of the cameras, egged on by the glamorous Barbara Kuhn, confessor to the stars. But the vacant Valley Girl visage of this nymphet symbolised, for him, the mass public he was trying to win over. Baum had convinced him that these first few days of the book's release were absolutely crucial. *The Fifth Gospel* was not the sort of publication that could be a sleeper, a slow burn. It must ignite the world's imagination in a coordinated campaign.

'My scrolls are the original deal,' said Theo, as captivatingly as he could, given that the girl was at that moment dabbing at the fleshy hollow between his nose and his upper lip. 'Malchus wrote his story directly on the papyrus with his own hand. And Malchus was *there*. When the Bible was happening, so to speak. He was in the garden of Gethsemane on the night Jesus was betrayed. He was the one who got his ear cut off.'

'Yeah?' A flicker of interest. 'I didn't know that. In this job, you learn something new every day. Yesterday, we had this other guy on the show. He's like the world's biggest expert on child abuse. And he's found a part of the brain where bad sex-related memories get stored. It's like a special part of the frontal load of the brain, he had diagrams of the exact location, and if you have an injection of some new kind of drug into that part, you can get rid of all the damage from the abuse. I was like: now *this* the world needs.'

'Speaking of which,' he quipped wearily, 'are you sure *I* really need so much make-up?'

'Relax,' she replied, with the aplomb of the very young. 'It's just to stop those big bad lights reflecting off of you. Otherwise you look like a total greaseball.'

On the scale of humiliations, Theo's appearance on the *Barbara Kuhn Show* was worse than some he'd endured in recent days, and better than others. Ms Kuhn had at least read the book, which was more than many chat-show hosts managed, despite the slimness of the text (126 pages, including Malchus's bits). She gave him a great intro — so good and so comprehensive, in fact, that there was little for him to add. There were only two logical directions to go after an intro like that: either he should be allowed to wave at the cameras, take a quick bow and leave, or he should be allowed to discuss Malchus's Gospel in-depth. Neither was on the agenda. This was TV, and he had to find a way of conveying the illusion of leisurely complexity in four minutes. The one mercy was that it was a pre-recorded affair, so there wasn't the ignominy of a horde of gum-chewing, applauding onlookers to contend with.

'Malchus was not a disciple as such, am I right?' said Ms Kuhn, whose ample chest was slightly wrinkled at close range but whose face was stretched flawless and inscrutable.

'Well, yes and no,' said Theo. 'Everyone who followed Jesus was a disciple, and Malchus certainly calls himself such. He's not one of the original twelve disciples Jesus chose. But then neither were Mark or Luke. Malchus actually met Jesus. He saw him crucified. He was there.'

The studio director, a stocky white-haired man in a black shirt and cream trousers, butted in from the sidelines. 'That's good, that's fine. But let's try not to have too many "yes and no" answers.'

'Do we have to do a retake?' said Theo.

'No, one "yes and no" is OK. One we can get away with. Just try not to do it again.'

'So,' rejoined Barbara Kuhn, 'Mr Grippin.'

Theo blinked. He hadn't yet fully adjusted to his nom de plume; each time journalists or talk-show hosts uttered it, his first instinct was to look over his shoulder to see whom they were addressing. But Baum had convinced him that 'Theo Griepenkerl' was a problem for customers and booksellers; the chances of somebody misspelling it in a search engine, or failing to remember it in the first place, were too high. 'Grippin' was nice and simple, yet distinctive enough to stand out in a crowded marketplace.

'A marketplace crowded with newly discovered Gospels?' Theo had remarked sarcastically.

Baum had shrugged. 'We can go with Griepenkerl if you insist. It's your call.'

Theo jerked back into focus, forced himself to re-inhabit the body that was perched on a cream sofa in the studio set of the *Barbara Kuhn Show*. His body was dressed in smart casuals, including a jacket he'd bought specially for this tour. His hair was washed and combed, the little scars on his face were hidden under a dusting of cosmetics. To the best of his ability, he switched on a light of amiable yet authoritative intelligence behind his eyes, for the viewers at home to notice and admire.

'Please, call me Theo,' he said.

'Tell me, Theo,' said Ms Kuhn. 'In what historical period exactly was Malchus writing?'

'Probably 38 AD, 40 AD, something like that.' Theo paused for a split second, in case the director demanded an exact date, then ploughed on. 'That's a full thirty to fifty years before the earliest of the New Testament Gospels is supposed to have been written, and just a few years after Christ's death. Basically, as soon as he's had his encounter with Jesus, Malchus quits his job as Caiaphas's spy and starts evangelising, and he does that full-on for several years, and then he gets a wasting disease that's presumably cirrhosis or cancer of the liver or something like that, and he writes his memoir.'

'Excuse me,' interjected the director again. 'But the narrative sequence is not too good here. This guy gets his disease after the career he has after meeting Jesus, but the viewers haven't even seen Jesus yet. If we could have more Jesus, and sooner, that would be excellent.'

'I think we should let Malchus speak,' said Theo, flipping the pages of *The Fifth Gospel* to the place he'd bookmarked. 'It's his words that are important, not mine. If you'll . . . ah . . . if you'll let me, I'd like to read the part where Jesus is in the garden of Gethsemane, and Judas has just betrayed him.' He lowered his eyes to the text, and tried not to appear fazed by the nearest camera rolling swiftly and silently towards him like a huge armour-plated predator. 'Malchus has been hanging around, gathering info for Caiaphas, the High Priest. Then this:

Upon the signal that was thus given by Judas, the soldiers moved forward. Only then was it evident to me that I, that is to say my body, was in the space between the Roman guards and the followers of Jesus. I counselled myself that I was in no danger, for the soldiers knew me to be the servant of Caiaphas, whereupon a servant of Jesus said, Lord, let me despatch these jackals. I was straight away upon my knees, believing a strong man had brought down his fist on my shoulder, with force enough to buckle my legs. In truth, as I was told afterwards, I was struck by a sword, which cut off the right ear from my head, so that it dangled to my shoulder like a woman's adornment.

Then Jesus stepped forth, and called to his servant to do no more, and furthermore Jesus said, I am a leader of a far mightier army than this.

Don't you think I could call down a battalion of
angels to fight for me? But the time is not yet.
Then bloody and giddy I fell forward, and my
face was upon his groin, and with gentle hands he
took my head——'

'Excuse me,' said the director. 'We have a problem.
Groin. Specifically: groin and Jesus. The *Barbara
Kuhn Show* is a mainstream show. We gotta be careful
with gay stuff. Johnny Mathis is fine. AIDS is OK,
within reason. Armani, Yves Saint Laurent . . . bring
'em on. But gay sex with Jesus . . .'

'I'm sure there's nothing sexual meant,' said Theo,
blinking into the spotlights. 'The groin is just
the . . . ah . . . relevant juncture of the body, that's
all. The bit where the . . . ah . . . lower torso meets
the legs. I could've translated it as "loin", but I felt
that would be unnecessarily archaic. See, in my translation, I wanted to strike a balance between the no-
nonsense directness of the original Aramaic and the
sort of weird Elizabethan-Hebrew hybrid that people
are used to from the King James——'

'Plus it's too long,' said the director. 'Way too long. This thing of reading aloud from a book on TV: it only works if you're an actor. I mean, like, an act-*tooor*.' And the director gestured in an extravagant fashion that struck Theo as, frankly, gay.

Barbara Kuhn, consummate professional that she was, perceived that the studio dynamic was growing slack and took it in hand.

'Let's talk about *you*,' she purred. 'How did you feel when you first set eyes on the scrolls?'

'Scared,' he said, wiping his powdered forehead nervously. 'Scared that another bomb would go off and I would be buried in the rubble of the Mosul museum's toilets.'

'Not to be found for another two thousand years,' suggested Ms Kuhn, deadpan.

He nodded, grinning like an idiot, relieved that she was steering the encounter back towards some kind of convivial conversation. Although, at the same moment, it dawned on him that she probably despised him, for some reason he would never guess unless he lived with her for half a decade.

'How long did it take you to translate the scrolls?'

'A few days. Maybe a week.'

'Only a week?'

He could tell from her tone that this was the wrong answer. And if he pointed out that the total amount of text was not large, he would only dig himself deeper, as it would imply that the book was flimsy. 'I'm fast,' he said. 'My Aramaic is probably as good as most people's French.'

'We'll need to cut that,' said the director. 'It would only make sense in Canada.'

'Sorry,' said Theo.

'We're not in Canada,' said the director, with a hint of peevishness.

'I appreciate that.'

'How did you feel, Theo,' Ms Kuhn pressed on, 'when you'd finished translating the scrolls?'

'Uh . . . I felt relieved. I felt I'd done a good job.'

'You didn't feel elated? A rush of excitement?' She was obviously trying to help him conform to a stereotype the viewers would find attractive.

'Pleased.' It was like the final offer in a haggling transaction.

'Uh-huh,' said Barbara Kuhn, and turned to face the camera, to touch base with her legions of supporters. 'Of course, what will astonish readers of this Gospel is the many differences between Malchus's version of events and the versions we know from the Bible. For example, there's a part where Malchus is in the garden of Gethsemane when Jesus has been betrayed by Judas, and one of the disciples slices off his ear with a sword . . .'

Theo nodded dumbly. He understood that this little précis of Ms Kuhn's meant that his carefully rehearsed, dramatic reading, freshly captured inside the cameras, was already condemned to oblivion.

'In the Bible,' continued Ms Kuhn, 'specifically in the Gospel of Saint Luke, who was a doctor, it says that Jesus reached out and healed Malchus's ear. But in Malchus's account, the ear isn't healed. Malchus goes home, gets his injury bandaged up, and it gets infected for a while – which he describes in great detail – and then finally it dries up. And for the rest of his life it's like a scrap of gristle hanging off the side of his head.'

'Or like a woman's adornment, as Malchus himself so vividly puts it,' said Theo.

'In other words,' Ms Kuhn pressed on, 'there's no miracle. Saint Luke made it up. He lied. How do you think Christians will feel about that?'

'Uh . . . well, interested, I hope.'

Ms Kuhn tilted her head to one side, a trademark gesture of mildly appalled bemusement that was selected for a close-up by the camera.

'What's your faith, Theo, if I may ask?'

'I don't have one.'

She leaned back, *faux*-reflective. 'If I could get you to imagine, if you will . . . If you *had* faith, how do you think you'd feel to read that Jesus's last words, on the cross, were not "It is finished" or "Into thy hands I commend my spirit", but "Please, somebody, please finish me"?'

'Uh . . . well, I hope it would give me a new awareness of Jesus's humanity, and the awfulness of what he went through.'

'Has it done that for you, Theo?'

Theo leaned back in his chair, fighting off a sensation of claustrophobia as beads of sweat broke through the make-up on his face and he saw his bloodshot eyes staring back at him from multifarious monitors and lenses.

'Yeah,' he breathed.

Judges

The Fifth Gospel had been out for six days, officially. Theo was, at this moment, chain-smoking and eating peanuts in a soulless corporate hotel in Los Angeles. The hotel room was the latest berth in his whistle-stop tour of the USA; the peanuts were provided in the mini-bar refrigerator, alongside various candies, savoury snacks and booze.

'Unbeatable deals on hair and nails,' chattered the TV, a hulking robot that loomed over the foot of the bed. Theo slid his fingers inside the foil sachet and fetched out another peanut. Each one tasted wonderful – lightly greased, salt-encrusted yet silky smooth – but there were too few of them in the packet. In fact, there were more peanuts depicted in the photo than actually inside the foil. There was also a helpful message for allergy sufferers: WARNING: CONTAINS NUTS.

'. . . five convenient locations,' the TV said. 'We're here waiting to welcome you!'

This seemed unlikely, given that it was now the middle of the night.

Theo opened the refrigerator and closed it again. The Elysium sales representative who'd chaperoned him earlier in the day had treated him to a Chinese buffet at 9 p.m., and there was no reason to feel ravenous now, especially since he would normally be asleep. He ought to have the willpower to limit his excess consumption to the sachet of peanuts. Face it, he did not *need* pretzels, Twinkie bars or Snickers-flavoured milk. In any case, the cost of all that crap would be added to the hotel bill, and somewhere down the line, weeks or months from now, a smart young accountant in Elysium's head office would peruse a list of all his expenses, peanuts and all. Printed on one balance sheet would be the number of copies sold of *The Fifth Gospel*; printed on another would be the author's attacks of the midnight munchies.

Of course, it was madness to worry about small change when hundreds of thousands of dollars had just taken up residence in his bank account. He should either pay for all the extras himself, or have the chutzpah to freeload with gusto. To his annoyance, he couldn't bring himself to do either.

He badly, badly, badly needed to know how well *The Fifth Gospel* was selling. All the sales reps in each city he visited assured him that the demand was phenomenal. The staff in all the bookstores told him the same. Shop window displays almost always found room to feature a copy, in amongst the latest bestsellers about sexy criminologists, celebrity footballers, loveable drug addicts, conspiracy theories, and the national trauma of 9/11 refracted with unbearable poignancy through a literary fable about an anorexic New York teenager and her imaginary friend Kuki. And, of course, Elysium's guide to teaching your kids arithmetic the *Sing Times Seven* way. The omens seemed excellent.

Yet he was aware that new books, movies and CDs are often launched in a haze of hoopla and that, when the haze clears, many items prove to have fizzled. Bargain bins and remainder tables are full of 'surefire sellers' and Next Big Things. Baum had done his utmost to make Theo feel that the $250,000 advance was a foolish, fatherly act of largesse, whose loss the publisher would bear with stoic good grace. Theo wanted to prove him wrong, to confirm that the sly old bastard was raking in the money.

Also, goddammit, *The Fifth Gospel* was Theo's first book and he should be excused for being desperate to know how it had been received in the world at large.

He took a swig from the can of Seven-Up he couldn't remember opening, to wash down the Twinkie bar he couldn't remember unwrapping. The digital numbers on the bedside clock had metamorphosed from 12:58 to 1:23. That was bad news. The amount of sleep he could hope to get if he went to bed and lost consciousness immediately had dwindled to five hours. At 6:30, he had to get up and catch a train to San Diego.

'A hand-tooled genuine cowhide leather sheath is included in the price if you order now!'

Theo pressed a button on the TV's remote control

to make the commercials go away. The screen reverted to a menu of the hotel's services. 24-hour internet access downstairs in the lobby was one of them.

Within ten minutes, Theo was seated in front of a PC, in a softly lit lounge overseen by bleary young Hispanics in livery. The only other guest was a Korean businessman with a fancy cellphone into whose mouthpiece he murmured constantly while typing at great speed. Whatever he was doing, it sure as hell wasn't browsing Amazon's book pages.

Theo typed his name into Amazon's search engine, and was instantly presented with:

Robert Griepenkerl: Das Schicksal eines freien deutschen Schriftstellers (Unknown Binding)
by *Ludwig Buttner* (Author)
No customer reviews yet. Be the first.

Grunting with irritation, he typed in 'Grippin' instead, which gave him:

**The Fifth Gospel: The Testament of Malchus,
The Lost Apostle (Hardcover)**
by *Theo Grippin* (Author)

Underscoring his name was a row of five stars, of
which two and a half had been filled in with gold.
The reviews of fifty-nine Amazon customers had
wrought this perfectly split average of approval and
disapproval. Did that mean that only fifty-nine
people had bought his book? No, of course it didn't.
At his Barnes & Noble gig yesterday in Fresno, he'd
seen, with his own eyes, twenty-odd people take
The Fifth Gospel to the cash registers.

Product details
Hardcover: 126 pages
Publisher: Elysium
Language: English
ISBN-13: 978 00073 13266
Product Dimensions: 9.3 x 6.1 x 0.7 inches
Amazon.com Sales Rank: 74 in Books

Seventy-four seemed a fantastically high ranking, compared to, say, 32,457, but these things could be deceptive. A book could shoot up the charts on the basis of a surge of orders from a single city. Maybe a dozen listeners to his radio interview on Fresno's KFSR yesterday had rushed to Amazon simultaneously, and their orders had impacted on Amazon's computer brain as evidence of heavy sales traffic, thus wildly boosting his rating in a temporarily captured window of time before the statistics regained their natural equilibrium.

Theo tried to forget about the numbers thing, and passed on to the product description.

Theo Grippin, leading expert in Biblical Aramaic (the language spoken by Jesus), has made the archaeological discovery of the century: nine papyrus scrolls written only a few years after Christ's crucifixion. Malchus, former servant of Jerusalem's high priest Caiaphas, is converted to the controversial new faith as a result of a person-to-person encounter with Jesus. He is an eyewitness at Calvary, one of the first to see the risen Christ, and a close associate of the apostles as they establish their infant church. Grippin relates the fascinating story of the scrolls and the challenges of translating them, but the heart of this book is Malchus's own account, as honest and vivid as when it was written – in the 1st century AD, at the dawn of the Western world's greatest faith.

Customers who bought this item also bought:

The Jesus Dynasty: The Hidden History of Jesus, His Royal Family, and the Birth of Christianity by James D. Tabor $10.88

The Da Vinci Code by Dan Brown $7.99

The Jesus Papers: Exposing the Greatest Cover-Up in History by Michael Baigent $10.85

The Lost Tomb of Jesus DVD $19.99

Theo frowned at the sight of these unwanted appendages to his own effort. A curse on these money-grubbing exercises in imaginary scholarship, cack-handed hokum and Mickey Mouse theology! He wished there was a more dignified, alternative version of Amazon that well-educated people could access, an Amazon where such trash was automatically filtered out. He felt like a classical conductor forced to share a stage with a bunch of simpering pop babes.

But the reviews: on to the reviews . . .

Julia Argandona, of Costa Mesa, CA, offered the following appreciation (which '17 of 59' customers apparently found 'helpful'):

I haven't read this book yet but I can't wait to read it so I am reviewing it early. The other people on Amazon who say don't read it are brainwashed stooges of the Catholic religion, which has been sexually abusing children for 100's of years. Who needs it? I already LOVE this book.

Ah, Julia Argandona, God bless her. Blind, un-
conditional support: what every author needs.
Although . . . there was no guarantee she would
approve of the book if and when she got around
to reading it. Still, it was a sale. Or was it? There
was no watertight proof of purchase to be divined
from the text.

A person identifying him/herself only as 'truth-
seeker' from East Coast, USA, had this to say:

> This book could have saved me a lot of money
> if it had been written earlier. If you've had
> questions all your life about who the miracle-
> working (not!) carpenter (not!) from Nazareth
> (not!) really was (or wasn't!), this is a perfect
> book to buy. But you might regret it because
> the truth hurts!

Couldn't ask for a better response from a blunt-
witted sort of reader, Theo supposed. Although
some specific mention of the book's content would
have been nice.

He got it, in spades, from the next reviewer, Frank R. Felperin (Sonoma, CA):

This book may be slim in volume but it is huge in importance. For here we have the first eye-witness account of New Testament events whose authorship is not problematical. The earliest documents in the New Testament are generally agreed to be Paul's letters, dictated to (and probably somewhat altered by) a scribe. They were written in Greek and Paul's experi-ence of Jesus was strictly inspirational, as he never met the man. Next chronologically are the Gospels and the Revelation of John, in disputed order of sequence, towards the end of the century. None of these are based on autographs and there is much evidence of tampering and outright invention. What is extraordinary about the memoir of Malchus is that it was written in Malchus's own hand, in Aramaic, only a few years after the crucifixion of Jesus.

There is, of course, a possibility that Theo Grippin is a fraudster whose claims about finding the scrolls are every bit as spurious as those peddled in the works of Baigent et al. But Grippin is a researcher and expert in Aramaic with impeccable academic credentials (detailed in an exhaustive appendix) and no prior record of catchpenny journalism. Moreover, the titles of his earlier forays into publication (eg, 'Some Anomalies In Post-Achaemenid Aramaic: Anti-Hellenism and Hebrew Hybrids') raise doubts that an intellect as dry as Grippin's could invent a memoir as garrulous and grotesque as Malchus's.

Among the remarkable contents of this account are:

1. Malchus attends the crucifixion, along with several of Jesus's disciples, who are obviously in shock. Jesus is naked and there is a spill of faeces down the vertical beam of the cross. Jesus also (unintentionally) urinates onto Malchus, who is standing nearer than the other

onlookers. Such details are likely to be extremely upsetting to many Christians.

2. Jesus's body, once dead, is allowed to hang on the cross for several days, as was usual in public crucifixions. Carrion-eating birds (whose precise species is unclear in the Aramaic, a detail on which Grippin expends a 17-line speculative footnote!) peck out his eyes and portions of his entrails.

3. There is no mention of Joseph of Arimathea or interment in the tomb. Jesus's mother (Miriam) and half a dozen other women (apparently well known to Malchus, but unnamed except for 'Rebekah' and 'Abishag') wait with Malchus on Golgotha in shifts. When the Roman soldiers finally dismantle the crosses of the executed men, and Jesus's corpse 'falls on the earth like a sack of flour', the group arrange a simple burial, the costs of which are borne by Malchus.

4. There is no mention of Resurrection in the commonly understood sense of that term.

Malchus and other supporters of Jesus have a vision or hallucination of him in restored health, as he was before his execution. Jesus does not speak, but makes gestures, the meaning of which is hotly debated among those who see them. After several weeks, during which the visions manifest more and more frequently among Jesus's disciples, a meeting is held. Malchus's normally sober, down-to-earth descriptive style is exchanged here for a rapturous, almost poetical meditation. It is therefore unclear what actually occurred, but the disciples emerge from the meeting in a state of elation and self-confidence. There are hints of drug use.

These and many other details have the potential to impact very negatively on Christianity as an institution. The fact that Malchus is a convert rather than a sceptic only makes his testimony more damaging, and Grippin's overlong forewords and afterwords, which give us no real clue as to his motives other than his passion for Aramaic, help to give the book an air of innocent authority.

Essential reading for anyone who wants to see what happens next in the troubled evolution of the Western world's most powerful religion.

Twenty-three of fifty-nine people apparently found Frank Felperin's review 'helpful', which, given the trouble Frank had gone to, seemed a tad ungenerous. But Theo could see, at a glance, that *The Fifth Gospel* was not universally admired:

I did not buy this book, so this author will not make a dime off me. I read it over a two day period in my local book store. The so-called gospel of Malchus is a blatant forgery produced by Muslims to undermine our faith. It's been tried before. When will they learn?

Thus spake K. Stefaniuk from Duluth, GA. Equally

dismissive was Boyd Benes from 'Toeldo' (presumably Toledo), Ohio:

> Save your money, this one is one big letdown. The real meat is thrity pages in the middle and the rest is just some acadmeic showing off what he knows about Aramanic, the language that Jesus supposely spoke. Grippen should have guiven this stuff yto a fiction writer to make something good out of it, instead he just gives it to you straight which I guess some peoples will admnire him for. But the guy, Malchius, is not that interesting. Once he gets his ear cut off and sees the crucifixtion, thats basicly it. And thats like page 50. Grippen needs to go back to where he found the scrtolls and try to dig up some more good stuff, enough for a book. But if he does, he will just write a secondf book instead of making this one what it should of been. I know how these authors operate.

Arnold P. Lynch from Wisconsin, promisingly billed as 'Biblical linguist', titled his review 'PITFALLS'. He did not waste time on a précis of *The Fifth Gospel*, nor did he feel obliged to mention any of the events described in the text, preferring to get straight down to his judicial summary:

As usual with ancient documents, the meddling of intermediaries and interpreters distorts the meaning. The word 'gospel' sets off alarm bells from the start, being a medieval term that has no place in a 1st century context. On the plus side, Malchus has some potentially valuable insights into the circumstances surrounding Yahshua's final days of corporeal incarnation but, you guessed it, Yahshua is mis-named Jesus throughout and his father is annoyingly referred to as God or even Lord instead of the proper Yahweh. This shows that Theo Grippin is an instrument of Satan, no better than the King James cabal. (Check out

the book's ISBN number: 1+3+2 66 = 666).
The Apostle Paul (before his words were
censored/disguised) said: 'Whosoever shall
call upon the name of Yahweh shall be saved'.
If you read the King James (per)version you
won't see the name Yahweh and if you don't
see it you can't call it and therefore can't be
saved. Clever! So, in conclusion, read this
book for the information but beware the traps
and pitfalls. Satan's hand is all over it.

Geraldine Des Barres, of Spanish Fork, Utah, raised
expectations in Theo of a Mormon slant on the
material, but merely said:

I started reading this book with an open mind
and quite interested in the topic. The first part
with Theo Grippen is quite good as you follow
him to Iraq and he gets bombed. But then it
became boring in the middle with this priest
type guy who has ulcers. That's when I put it
down and didn't pick it back up. Maybe if I

had read to the end it would have got better. Usually writers try and make sure there is a big climax at the end but Theo Grippen is a first timer so, who knows. Maybe Dan Brown will write a fictional novel based on this book and it will be a blockbuster.

Charles 'Book Muncher' Volman, under the mysterious heading 'JOYCE IS THE MAN!', added:

Theo Grippin claims to have discovered an accoubt by an eye witness to Jesuss' crucifixtion. And the way the eye witness descirbes it, there is no way Jesus could have survived, he is 100% dead. Which is 100% proof that this book is a big fat fake. (Well, not so fat — it is only 120 pages) The fact that Jesus SURVIVED has been common knowledge in esoteric circles for hundreds of years, and finally documented beyonf doubt in The Jesus Scroll by Donovan Joyce (New American Library, 1972, tragically out of print). JOYCE

IS THE MAN! As for Grippin he is just trying
to cash in on the current success of Jesus
stories. The true facts are in danger of loosing
all credibilty every time another book like this
comes out. I mean, whats next, Jesus was a
woman and he went to Norway and joined the
vikinmgs? Give me a break.

Stephanie Geitner in Cincinnati took a more philo-
sophical stance, and generously donated two stars,
despite her lofty condescension towards Theo's
effort:

The man who wrote this thinks he has found
something that was hidden for two thousand
years. In truth, nothing is found or not found
unless God wills it. The word of God cannot
be lost nor can it be excavated by accident.
The accounts preserved in the Bible were
chosen by Jesus to be his mouthpiece for the
2000 years between his crucifixion and today.
Any documents that have been found since,

whether they be the Dead Sea Scrolls, the so-called Gospel of Judas, or this so-called Gospel of Malchus, come to light only because God has a purpose for them at the time. I do not know what the purpose of *The Fifth Gospel* is, but God is in control, and Theo Grippin is an instrument of the Lord whether he believes it or not. Every word he writes, not to mention every breath he breathes, is made possible by the Supreme Intelligence that allows his fingers to move upon a keyboard or hold a pen. Christians, do not fear this man's book. All is revealed that needs to be revealed, and all is hidden that needs to be hidden.

'Your croissant and coffee are *ready*, sir.'

It was the third time the words had been spoken, but Theo hadn't registered until now that they were addressed to him. The sultry woman behind the bar was keeping her voice low, in deference to the late hour, but she had broken his trance by sounding just a little pissed off.

'Uh . . . thanks, I'll be there in a second,' Theo replied. He wanted to read just one more review. It was kind of addictive, despite being so unpleasant and unsatisfying.

Tessa Bawden, who didn't say where she was from, kept her feedback short and sweet:

Mr Grippin, before I read your book I was saved and steadfast in the Lord. I thought Jesus was holding me in his arms like a baby. Now I am lost and alone. I can see that Jesus was just like me and nothing more, ie, a bunch of bones and guts covered in skin. We all wish there was more and we build a dream of heaven on those wishes, but when the heart stops, that's the end of the dream. In my life as a Christian I had lots of arguments with atheists and read lots of anti-Christian books and my faith remained strong. It's funny that poor little Malchus, who loved Jesus so much, and you, who don't seem to have any agenda that I can see, should be the ones to turn off the Light of my life. Actually, it's not funny at all. Did you spare any thought for people like me before you gave your book to the world? I bet you didn't. Enjoy your money, Mr Grippin, and everything else your success brings you. Thanks for nothing.

More Than Heart Could Wish

'Good morning,' said the voice on the other side of the door. 'Room service.'

Theo looked at Jennifer in the bed next to him, in case she shook her head in dissent or lurched sideways to retrieve her clothes. She nodded languidly. Her only concession to privacy was to pull the sheets up over her naked breasts.

'Come in.'

The hotel employee was a female too. She didn't bat an eyelid at the sight of the bigshot author in bed with the gorgeous blonde who, only yesterday afternoon, had cordially introduced herself to him, with a handshake, in the hotel lobby.

'Two freshly squeezed orange juices, two coffees, toast with egg over easy, toast with egg sunny side up, two blueberry muffins, two messages, and . . . uh . . . a CD by John Coltrane.'

It was true. All these things were on the silver tray.

Theo had ordered the breakfast but not the CD. Even from halfway across the room, he recognised its cover photo. Amazed, he looked down at Jennifer for an explanation.

'The magic of credit cards,' she murmured, with a mischievous grin. 'And couriers.'

They breakfasted in bed, basking in the warmth of the sun streaming through the balcony window. Jennifer's laptop played Coltrane's *Stellar Regions* through its inbuilt speaker, at quite robust volume and with decent sound quality. Every now and then there was a slight stutter in the reproduction but, given the semi-abstract nature of the material, nothing to spoil Theo's enjoyment.

'You better be careful around me,' said Jennifer, her eyes twinkling in the shadow of her teased and tousled fringe. 'Whatever you mention is on your mind, I might just make it happen.'

'So I've noticed,' he said. The room, large though it was, smelled of sex, and there were two squishy condoms discarded at the side of the bed, one from last night and one from earlier this morning. Jennifer had provided the condoms as well.

'This is very thoughtful of you,' he said.

'Oh, I love this album too,' she said. 'I was *so* in the mood to hear it again.'

She wiped her buttery fingers on the bedsheet and picked up the CD case. It was a Digipak, so she could hold it open like a miniature book as she sipped her coffee. Coltrane, immaculately dressed as always in his purple suit, gazed up from the chiaroscuro depths, poised to blow his saxophone.

'You're still number one,' she said.

Theo wasn't sure if she was addressing Coltrane or himself.

'In the *New York Times*,' she added. 'Second week running.'

'How do you know?'

'I checked emails as I was loading in the CD.'

'I didn't notice. You must have done it when I blinked.'

'Yeah, I'm quick.' She said it matter-of-factly, as if it was part of her job.

Theo read the two messages that the hotel reception staff had deposited on his breakfast tray. They were both from literary agents. One greeted him with a bit of modern Aramaic – *Šlama 'loxun!* – before making her pitch. He had to give her points for trying. Her name was Zarah Obatunde and she sounded terribly young.

'Sounds terribly young, doesn't she?' remarked Jennifer. Her eyes were pointed elsewhere and he couldn't understand how she'd managed to read Ms Obatunde's message.

'Yes,' he said.

'You'll get a lot of those,' she said.

Theo read the other message, which was from Martin F. Salati, an agent who'd written to him three times before, at various intervals on this tour.

'This guy is kind of my stalker,' said Theo.

'I know him,' said Jennifer. 'Marty Salati. He's good. A pro.'

'Maybe I need an agent.'

'It's a bit late now.' She made a motion in the air with her slender hand, like a priest issuing a blessing.

After a moment, he realised she'd mimed the signing of a contract.

'Anyway,' she continued, 'it hardly matters. You've done very well, Theo. I don't think it's hit you yet what's happened with this book. You are, shall we say, on a level very few authors ever get to. You are . . .' words failed her, for a moment, '*way* up there.' And she threw her arm up at the ceiling. The bedclothes slipped off her breasts again.

Theo mopped up the last of the egg yolk with a scrap of toast. Coltrane's sax and Rashied Ali's drums skittered around the bridal suite, chasing each other up the walls, along the ceiling, under the curtains, and out onto the balcony, where they leapt into the humid sky of Baltimore.

Theo liked Baltimore. It was supposed to be very dangerous, but he liked it. And he liked the Harborfront Hotel particularly. It had been a rat-infested banana warehouse right up until the 1970s, then been transformed into a gleaming citadel of luxury accommodation. Yet the staff weren't snooty; everyone was very nice to him, very laid-back. Well, everyone except that crazy Filipina cleaning lady, who had reproached him in broken English yesterday, weeping and shaking her mop. He hoped she hadn't lost her job over it. Disliking a book shouldn't be a crime, and anyway, with *The Fifth Gospel* at number one on the bestseller list for the second week in a row, he could afford to be forgiving.

'When do I have to get on the train for Philadelphia?' he asked Jennifer.

'Twelve thirty-five,' she said without hesitation. 'But we can change it for a plane leaving at three p.m., if you like. Your gig at Borders isn't until eight thirty.'

'I thought I might like to have a wander around the city.'

'I can get you anything you want, delivered here,' she said.

'Thanks, but I feel like stretching my legs.'

She stroked his thigh through the bedsheets. 'Mmm, you're good at that.'

Stellar Regions had reached the title track, and encountered a digital hiccup. Coltrane's sax repeated the same note in rapid-fire succession, then moved on.

'This is my favourite cut,' Jennifer said. 'Awesome.'

'Yes, but now that Alice Coltrane is dead, they should correct the title, don't you think?' He couldn't believe he was testing her like this; it was the sort of question Meredith would have rolled her eyes at. But the circumstances of his life had changed so much in the last couple of weeks that he felt a little mistrustful of his marvellous fortune. Jennifer was kind of a final straw, fortune-wise. You get introduced to your latest Elysium representative in your latest city, and she's not the usual author escort or uninformed underling, but a Senior Editor, and she's beautiful and smart and she loves jazz, and within a few hours she's in bed with you. The notion that, on top of all that, she should be genuinely au fait with the controversial provenance of John Coltrane's *Stellar Regions* seemed too good to be true.

'I don't know,' she replied. 'Does it make all that much difference whether it's called "Stellar Regions" or "Venus"? Who knows what John would have called it if he'd lived?'

'"Venus", I bet,' he said. 'And maybe he wouldn't even have put the album out.'

'So we have Alice to thank,' said Jennifer. 'She released it, you love it, I love it, so everyone's happy, right?'

'Hmm,' he said. 'I've never been sure about the string overdubs.' (It wasn't true: he'd always *loved* the strings. Why the hell was he playing devil's advocate now?) 'Putting strings and Indian instruments all over a track that was originally recorded just by the four guys . . . I dunno.'

'John and Alice were partners,' Jennifer reminded him. 'In love and in art. He was behind her one hundred per cent of the way.'

Theo slumped back against his pillow. He had lost his will to spar with her, or maybe she'd just passed the test. 'Yeah. I suppose the best solution would be to put the undoctored recordings on an expanded issue of the CD, as bonus tracks. Then everybody could make up their own minds.'

'Sure,' she said. 'Maximum choice. Always good.'

He slipped out of bed and walked over to the jacuzzi, considered it, then passed on to the shower cubicle, where he shut himself in and turned the dial.

The torrent of hot water was just what he needed. He let it flow over his face for a couple of minutes. He tore open the complimentary sachet of shampoo and lathered his hair, noting, as always, the bald area of scalp under his soapy fingers. He rubbed cleansing froth onto his hairy abdomen, noting, as always, the total lack of what lifestyle magazines called 'abs'. He was an average guy with average defects. Jennifer was an alpha female, even more streamlined and perfect naked than when she was clothed. This was what a number one bestseller did for you. This was what you earned along with the money.

'There's no need to upgrade to a plane,' he told her a few minutes later when he was towelling himself dry. 'I just want a short walk, is all. A half hour, maybe. Just to get some sun, look at the people on the streets. I'll be ready for the Philadelphia train by midday.'

She had made good use of his time in the shower. Her hair was neatly reshaped, her lipstick glossy, her body tightly wrapped in a pencil skirt, fresh white blouse and chamois jacket. A list of emails glowed on her laptop screen, and *Stellar Regions* had come to an end.

'I'll come with you,' she said.

'You don't need to, honestly.'

'Indulge me, please. I like you, but I like my job too, and my job is to make sure you get to your gig in Philadelphia safe and sound.'

He hitched up his underpants, embarrassed at the way the waistband seemed to underline his protuberant gut.

'I don't get it,' he said. 'Surely my public appearances are less and less important with each day that goes by? I mean, the book is a huge success. Everybody knows about it, and the ones that don't will hear about it regardless of what I do. So . . . let's pretend – I mean, I wouldn't do this, but let's pretend I went to a bar in Baltimore and got plastered and missed my reading in Philadelphia. Would it make any difference?'

Jennifer leaned over and kissed him on the cheek with her luscious little lips.

'Go easy on the hubris, lover,' she cooed.

Theo strolled along Baltimore's harbour, licking an ice cream. Jennifer walked beside him, carrying his plastic bag of purchases (a glossy photography tome about the city's past, which he planned to send to his mother for her birthday; several Rahsaan Roland Kirk CDs; a shirt). The bag was heavy on her thin wrists and she switched it from hand to hand as she walked, transferring her cellphone from ear to ear as she took calls from various colleagues.

It was a brilliant day. Families with children were out in force, not just in the shopping areas but even on the surface of the water, floating happily to and fro in dinghies shaped like Disneyland sea serpents. A one-man band paraded up and down the jetty, fingering his accordion, tooting on his trumpet contraption, clashing the cymbals tied to his knees. Theo pointed to a flurry of movement under a nearby garbage can: a duck and duckling, huddled together, wings interleaved.

'Wow,' he said. 'They're real.'

'You were expecting . . . ?' she said.

'I mean, they've managed to survive in amongst all this hustle-bustle. You'd think it would freak them out.'

'They're highly motivated, I'm sure.' As if to prove her point, the over-filled garbage can spontaneously jettisoned some of its topmost contents: several bucks' worth of crab.

'Wow,' Theo said again. Even when he'd been led past the scene, he kept turning around to check whether the ducks were still there.

'If they can't get their ca-ca together, I think we should just go elsewhere,' said Jennifer. She was talking to somebody on the phone. 'There are other distributors working 24/7. They'll guarantee fulfilment even if it means FedEx planes. So why do we let these clowns keep crying on our shoulder about trucks stuck in traffic jams? I mean, God, this is *books* we're talking about, not steel girders.'

Theo had finished his ice cream. His lips were sticky with chocolate. Jennifer, still talking, jammed her cellphone between her jaw and shoulder, and extracted a small item from her jacket pocket. She handed him what at first appeared to be a condom foil but proved, when torn open, to contain a moist towelette.

'Baum?' said Jennifer into her cellphone. 'Don't worry about Baum. He's a sweetie but he's . . .' She reached over to Theo and helped him wipe a smudge of chocolate he'd missed, on his cheek. 'Things are moving out of Mr Baum's . . . ah . . . sphere. He knows it too; it's no secret. How can I put this? I think you'll find that when the Ocean deal takes proper effect, these sorts of . . . ah . . . consultations will no longer be necessary. Does that . . .? Good. Good. Any time. That's what I'm here for.'

A few minutes later, on the East Pratt Street pier, Jennifer and Theo stood admiring the magnificent old power plant which had been converted into a Barnes & Noble superstore. Theo had performed there last night but it had been dark and Jennifer had ushered him straight from the taxi into the building. He'd noted the splendid aquarium with its giant-sized angel fish, and the clever way some of the smoke stacks had been converted into bookshelves, but only a small part of his mind had been open to these things; the demands of the gig had preoccupied him. He was not a natural performer, which made the pressure of reading aloud more onerous, especially since audience response to Malchus tended to include gasps, mutterings and exclamations. After the question-and-answer session and the signing, he'd been so emotionally drained that he wanted nothing more than for Jennifer to take him back to his hotel.

Today, observing the book emporium-cum-power station from a distance, he appreciated what an impressive piece of architecture it was. Although built for no more exalted purpose than to generate electricity, it had the dark grandeur of a cathedral.

A giant phallic guitar, in honour of a Hard Rock Cafe franchise within, penetrated the azure sky like a steeple.

'Excuse me,' said a voice from below. 'You're Theo Grippin, aren't you?'

He looked down. A black woman in a wheelchair was smiling up at him. She was fat and ugly and dressed in bright yellow sportswear, with fore-shortened legs that ended in sheepskin booties. Her eyes were likewise bright yellow.

'You did a reading in there last night,' she said, jerking her head towards Barnes & Noble.

'That's right,' said Theo. 'Were you there, ma'am? I didn't see you.'

'I wasn't there,' she said. 'I wanted to be, but I got this here wheelchair, and that building is too difficult.' She pronounced the final syllable with a definite 'kult' emphasis, the way lower-class Americans often do.

'I'm sorry to hear that,' said Theo.

'Can we help you, ma'am?' said Jennifer.

'I read your book, Mr Grippin,' said the black

woman, eyes fixed unswervingly on Theo. '*The Fifth Gospel.*'

'Oh, thank you,' he said.

'No need to thank me, Mr Grippin,' said the black woman. 'God told me to read it. It was very innaresting.'

'Uh . . . I'm glad you thought so.'

'I would appreciate it so much if I could have your autograph. I got a special autograph book.'

'Uh . . . I'd be happy to.'

She fumbled inside her polyester garments with her stubby fingers. Instinctively, Theo bent down towards her, ready to oblige when she pulled her autograph book to light.

Instead, she pulled out a handgun. It loomed into the space between her and Theo, so potent and frightening it might as well have been fired already. She lifted the grey metal barrel towards his forehead.

'You done an evil thing, Mr Grippin,' she said, more in sadness than in anger. 'You goin' straight to Hell.'

Theo's vision blurred; his heart beat too loud and too hard to spare much blood for his brain. *I'm not ready*, he wanted to say, but there would be no time for words.

'Put it down, ma'am.' Jennifer's voice, echoing in the void.

Theo swayed on his feet, and the black woman's face swam back into focus. A second gun had materialised in the space between them. One was pointing at his chest, but wavering. The other was pointing at the black woman's face, the tip of its barrel jammed against the bridge of her nose, nudged into the hollow of her eye. A delicate white hand held this gun; an elegantly manicured finger was wrapped round the trigger; a slim wrist kept the weapon steady.

'Put it away, ma'am,' said Jennifer.

The black woman did as she was told.

'Now get moving.'

The black woman took one last look at Theo, immolating him with a glower of hate. Then, in silence, she clamped her hands on the tyres of her wheelchair, swivelled roughly around, and rode away. Her wheels squeaked along the waterfront.

Theo dropped to his knees, coughed a couple of times, then spewed a soupy mixture of Pepsi and chocolate ice cream. He felt Jennifer's hand on his back.

'I'm sorry, I'm sorry,' he moaned.

'Nothing to be sorry for,' she said.

He looked up at her. She was amazingly, horribly calm.

'I . . . I guess I'm not used to guns,' he said.

'This is Maryland,' she said. 'Everybody's got one here.'

She had already returned her weapon to wherever she'd concealed it before. Theo couldn't imagine a cavity in her snugly tailored clothing where a hunk of steel could be stashed away without causing a bulge, but it was done.

He shuddered, retched again. It was extraordinary how visceral an effect it could have on you, being threatened with a gadget you'd seen a million times for entertainment. In the movies, heroes under fire were always galvanised into action, leaping around athletically or standing firm, as though bullets were tennis balls to be fielded or ignored. Theo felt like he'd been blasted open. The vomit on his chest felt like blood. He wiped at it ineffectually.

'Hey,' said Jennifer, waggling his bag of purchases. 'It's a good thing you bought a new shirt.'

He hung his head. Her self-possession was not in the least reassuring; it made him feel worse. She should be on her knees sobbing, or having hysterics, and he should be comforting her, or snapping her out of it with a slap to the face.

'Doesn't anything faze you?' he asked.

'Sure I'm fazed,' she said. 'I'm only human. But we've all got to perform, haven't we?' She ran one hand through her hair, in a slightly trembly gesture that might have been a stress reaction, except that she managed to take a quick peek at her wristwatch while doing so. 'We've both had a shock. Let's go back to the hotel and get over it together.'

He nodded. But the nod wasn't really assent, it

was just a reflex. He didn't want to be in a hotel room with Jennifer. Ever again. He wanted to get the hell out of Baltimore, which was a bad place full of bad people. He wanted to be on a train, in an otherwise empty compartment, watching a blurry landscape through the window, on a wonderfully slow journey that took hours and days and weeks and never arrived in Philadelphia.

'Tell you what,' said Jennifer. 'Let's get you there fast. I'll make one call, and you can fly.'

The Multitudes

'I hope Jennifer took good care of you,' said Tomoko Steinberg, with a hint of a smile, as she led him from Arrivals towards the John F. Kennedy car park. She was a petite Japanese, the epitome of ironic-chic in her vintage 1980s T-shirt emblazoned with FRANKIE SAY: RELAX. It was about four sizes too big for her, fulfilling the function of a dress, and the white cotton contrasted nicely with her brocaded red pantyhose. Her calf-length boots were pure white, but supple and wrinkled as if she'd worn them day and night for years. She was in her late forties and looked twenty-five; the search engine Theo had consulted yesterday had identified her as the widow of a famous sculptor.

'Yes, please,' said Theo. 'I mean, yes, thank you.' He laughed wearily as he stumbled along beside her through the airport lounge. He was beyond tired.

'You are beyond tired, aren't you?' she said, steering him gently out of the path of a posse of Brazilian tourists pushing high-velocity luggage trolleys.

'I could sleep for a week.'

'One good night will probably do it,' she said. 'You'll have a comfortable bed, I promise.'

'Oh, so Jennifer told you about the nightmare hotel in Philadelphia?'

The accommodation in Philly had been a second-floor room in an opulent, prestigious establishment, facing out onto the main street. A small group of protesters had stood underneath his window, serenading him with Christian songs and abuse. Jennifer's attempts to distract him with carnal delights had failed, and he'd slunk off to his bookstore appearance in a wretched state. And when he'd returned to the hotel, Jennifer suddenly announced she had to take a late plane back to Baltimore ('Something's come up') and that she would catch up with him in Boston, maybe. He'd lain in bed alone, in a litter of miniature booze bottles, staring up into a haze of his own smoke, listening to the protesters. Those religious people never knew when to quit.

'Nightmare hotel?' echoed Tomoko Steinberg.

'It was . . . ah . . . kind of noisy.'

'My authors don't sleep in hotels when they come to New York,' she assured him. 'They sleep at our house.'

By 'our house', she presumably meant the former Steinberg studio, which had been converted into the Manhattan office of Ocean Group, the multimedia company that was currently in the throes of a merger with Elysium.

'I don't want to cause any trouble.'

She chuckled, revealing a gold tooth. 'You gotta admit that's funny,' she said. 'In the circumstances.'

The Steinberg abode, although located in a stratospherically expensive part of Manhattan, was smaller and funkier than Theo expected. A friendly young intern called Heather let them in the door, with such unguarded casualness that the electronic sensors, massive steel lock and triple-thick glass didn't seem especially fearsome or obstructive, but merely quaint eccentricities of the building that the residents had learned to humour.

The ground floor, an open-plan hive of modest dimensions painted sky blue and decorated with avant-garde memorabilia, was buzzing with congenial activity, most of it centred around slim-line computers and scanner/printers. A grainy black and white poster of a young Philip Glass playing electronic organ for a tiny audience at the Film Makers' Cinematheque had pride of place near the window; the window-bars threw a neat pattern of shadows on it. Phones flashed constantly but were rarely answered; the prevailing noise was the musical hubbub of young people's *sotto voce* conversation.

'Coffee and stuff,' Tomoko called over her shoulder as she motioned Theo into the elevator. 'Please.'

'I don't know if I can go through with this,' groaned Theo, sinking ever deeper into the couch which the illustrious Bill Steinberg had often sunk into and which, despite cigarette burns and epoxy spatters, had been allowed to remain.

'Go through with what?'

'Tonight.'

'You'll be fine,' said Tomoko. She knelt on the plush Berber rug and began to tease her Pomeranian with a rolled-up magazine. 'By tomorrow morning it will be a memory. And you've got a two-day break before Boston.'

'I kept telling myself it was kind of fun,' he reflected. 'Until I got threatened with the gun.'

'Poetry,' she said, and snorted. 'No, I'm sympathetic, truly. It must have been awful for you.'

'Every reading I do, there seem to be more and more crazy people in the audience.'

Mrs Steinberg was on her elbows and knees now, making eyes at the dog. 'Well, it *is* a mindfuck of a book,' she said, in between inarticulate noises of motherly affection. 'You must have known that when you wrote it.'

At this angle, Theo couldn't see the expression on her face, only the gusset of her pantyhose. He looked wildly around the room, fighting back an attack of paranoia. Nothing could harm him here; he was among good-humoured, intelligent, supportive people, in a cosy loft where great art had once been made. He had a cup of perfectly brewed filter coffee in one hand and a cookie in the other. There were interesting expressionist paintings on the walls by talented youngsters, a few carved African statuettes, Japanese ornaments. The Pomeranian was cute and well behaved. All was calm, calm, calm.

'The parts that freak people out are Malchus's parts,' he said. 'I'm not responsible for those.'

She turned to face him, letting her dog take possession of the prize. 'You're too modest,' she said. 'Malchus is brilliant. A totally brilliant creation.'

There was a pause. The Pomeranian, whose name was Tipp-Ex, laid its soft little head on the rolled-up magazine and closed its eyes.

'I didn't make Malchus up,' said Theo. 'He's real.'

'That's totally how it comes across,' said Tomoko Steinberg admiringly.

'You don't understand,' explained Theo. 'I'm

serious. I really did find those scrolls. I really did translate them from Aramaic into English. Malchus, Jesus, the crucifixion . . . it's all true.'

She stared at him, her lips slightly parted in bemusement. 'Wow,' she said, in dawning recognition of the hidden value of her company's investment. 'That makes it even *better*.'

What might have been an awkward, even ugly scene between them was somewhat rescued by the urgent necessity of cooperating to pick up the shards of broken glass from the carpet. He'd thrown his coffee cup towards the nearest wall, and hit a drinks cabinet instead. Neither of them wanted to summon an Ocean employee upstairs to deal with this mess. So, without speaking, they crawled gingerly on their knees, inch by inch, fetching up the sharp fragments between their fingertips and transferring them into an empty ice bucket. For a long time there was no sound in the loft but their slow, regular breathing, the faster breathing of Tipp-Ex, and the soft clunk of glass against metal.

The larger shards were soon collected, but a ridiculous number of tiny splinters still clung to the fibres of the Berber. Theo and Tomoko had to be careful not to slice open their fingertips on those. They *were* careful. Their mutual care was a kind of intimacy; it bonded them, sort of.

'I'm sorry,' said Theo.

'Don't mention it. I've seen worse. Believe me, whatever you can do, I've seen worse.'

'From other authors?'

'Yes. And from my husband. Saint Bill Steinberg, God's gift to the plastic arts. Critics always said he attacked his sculptures rather than carved them, which was pretty accurate, but clay wasn't the only thing he attacked.'

'Thanks, that makes me feel just great.'

She smiled indulgently. 'Let's concentrate on getting you through the next ten hours or so. Then you'll be in bed. And tomorrow morning you'll be a new person.'

They'd reached the point where the remaining particles of glass were too small for fingers to retrieve.

'Is there a vacuum cleaner?' asked Theo.

'I don't think so.'

'No vacuum cleaner, in a house like this?'

'We have a cleaner,' she said. 'I mean a *human* cleaner. She comes every day at ten thirty for an hour. She brings her own equipment.'

Tomoko took hold of the corners of the rug and gathered the whole thing into her arms. It looked like a dead goat. She walked over to the window, swung it open, and began to shake the rug out into the air.

'Isn't that dangerous, maybe, for anyone down below?' asked Theo.

'We're three storeys up,' she replied, unconcerned. 'The wind will take care of it.'

At the reading, there were as many people crowded into the bookstore as New York's fire regulations permitted, plus two or three extra. It was the biggest crowd the staff had seen since J.K. Rowling. Theo was hiding in the staffroom, staring into a glass of wine that he balanced on his lap. There were four or five people in the room with him; he wasn't sure of the exact number because he was doing his best to keep his attention focused on his own lap, and he had already forgotten the names attached to the hands he'd shaken.

He wondered if he was already experiencing the effects of the pill Tomoko had given him just before the taxi ride, or if he was merely going crazy. The pill had been small and orange, dispensed from an unmarked plastic pot. 'It's an herbal pick-me-up,' she'd assured him, pronouncing 'herbal' in the American way, 'erbil'. It had recalled to his mind a heated argument he'd once had with Meredith about the linguistic idiocy of the usage 'an historical'. The recollection of the Theo/Meredith argument had filled his head, leaving no room for a considered decision as to the pros and cons of taking the pill. Even now, as he felt his insides straying out of his skin and wandering unsupervised around the room, all he could think of was another riposte to his long-gone girlfriend: 'You wouldn't say "an heated argument", would you?'

'Pher-*naar*-menal,' said the event organiser, a sasquatch of a man in a Pixies T-shirt. 'Pher-*naar*-menal.'

This guy, whose name Theo kept forgetting, was a fount of information about the fame and success of *The Fifth Gospel*. This fount he kept pouring into Theo's head, in order to pass the time until the scheduled start of the event.

'You are on course to pass *Gone With The Wind*,' he said.

'Pass?' echoed Theo.

'Twenty-eight million copies out there.'

'Out there?'

The event organiser spread both hands, to indicate the marketplace in all its vastness.

One of his colleagues was sceptical. 'You are slightly full of shit, bro,' he remarked. 'No book sells more than two million in America in a year.'

The Pixies guy rose to the bait. 'I used the words "out there", Matt. "Out there" does not mean books sold to customers, nor does it mean America alone. I'm talking worldwide and I'm including advance orders and I'm looking at how many copies will be in stock worldwide by the end of this year, in bookstores from Amsterdam to Zagreb.'

'You can't know that,' said Matt. 'It's sheer guess-work.'

'Guesswork based on hard figures. OK, I know these are not firm sales. And there might be a ton of returns. I doubt it, though. I seriously doubt it.'

Tomoko Steinberg, who appeared to know the organiser well, chipped in: 'But the true picture is better than that. The *Gone With The Wind* figures represent the total number of copies sold, since original publication. And that book came out, like, *whenever*. Ancient times.'

'The thirties,' said the Pixies guy. 'Sure, the figures are misleading. *You* think they underrate the perform-ance of *The Fifth Gospel*; Matt thinks they overrate. Thing is, I'm trying to give Mr Grippin an idea of the ballpark. Like, another example, *Uncle Tom's Cabin*. Twenty-eight million also. And that came out in 1852. By the end of this year, or a couple years max, Mr Grippin, I estimate you will have sold what Harriet Beecher Stowe took a century and a half to sell. That's what we're dealing with here.'

'Amazing,' said Theo. There was a mote of dust

in his wine, catching the light of the fluorescent bulb overhead. He agitated the glass slightly, to see the bright speck twirl in the red liquid.

'We got a ways to go yet before we top *Harry Potter* and *Lord Of The Rings*,' said the Pixies guy. 'I'm not suggesting we'll ever do that. But I think we might top *Code*. Given time.'

A female employee ducked back into the room, having had a peek at the assembled multitude.

'A nice mix,' she said. 'All colours, all ages. Well, no kiddies. But this is not *Harry Potter*.'

'It's the work of Malchus, a man in the first century AD,' said Theo, addressing his wine. 'It's not my book. It's his. Let's get that straight.'

'*You* gave it to the world, Mr Grippin,' said the young female. She was obviously a nice person. She wore a crisp white shirt and looked fresh and sincere. Before he could stop himself, Theo pictured her on her knees, sucking his dick with porn-star efficiency.

'I'm starting to regret it,' he said.

'Relax,' said Tomoko. 'People *like* to be stirred by a book. They may act upset, but they love it really.

It makes a change from all the forgettable, mindless entertainment that we consume the rest of the time.'

'Hey, I just thought of the perfect comparison,' the Pixies guy butted in, happily inspired. '*Lord Of The Rings*, *Code*, they're not the same kind of exercise as *The Fifth Gospel*. They're make-believe. What we got here is a true life account, more or less. Like Dave Pelzer's *A Child Called "It"*. People think that book sold mega. It sold good, but it didn't set the world on fire. You know how much that book sold, in paperback, in an average year? Not twenty-eight million. Not two point eight million. Under 700 thousand. *Under 700 thousand.* Just think about that, friends. True life account. Misery. Mass media interest. Author willing to tour his ass off. Seven hundred K.'

'I thought *A Child Called "It"* was horseshit,' said the fresh-faced female, puncturing the illusion of her innocence in Theo's eyes. 'I didn't buy it.'

'You got it for free,' teased Matt.

'No, I mean I thought his so-called life story was highly . . . uh . . . *massaged*. Whereas I don't get that with Malchus.'

Matt nodded. 'Yeah, Malchus is in a class up from Dave Pelzer. He's more . . . Anne Frank.'

'Twenty-five million copies,' said the Pixies guy without missing a beat. 'Worldwide sales since 1947. Like Matt says: like for like. And we're on course to leave *Anne Frank* way behind by the end of this year. What was your advance, Mr Grippin, if you don't mind me asking?'

'I forget,' said Theo, hypnotised by the mote of dust, which he imagined as an infinitesimally small dolphin trapped in a stagnant inlet.

'He was robbed, that's all I'm at liberty to tell you,' said Tomoko Steinberg. 'If he'd come to Ocean first off, we would have done him proud.'

'Hey, it just occurred to me,' said Matt. 'Mr Grippin?'

'Hmm?'

'The scrolls. Where are they now?'

'Now?'

'Where are you keeping them? The original papyruses?'

Theo lifted his wine to his mouth and took a

deep swig. He would have to snap into focus soon, to face the public.

'Papyri,' he said. 'And they're in my apartment.'

'Not in a secret bank vault?'

Theo smiled wearily. 'It's only in Dan Brown novels and conspiracy theories that documents get stored in secret bank vaults. This is real life.'

'Well, I don't know, Mr Grippin, but in real life, in New York, if you had a bunch of amazingly valuable documents in your apartment and you went away on tour, sure as hell there'd be all sorts of people doing their best to break into your place and steal 'em.'

'Canada,' said Theo. 'I live in Canada.'

'With all due respect, Mr Grippin, being Canadian is not a magic charm against anything bad that might happen to a person.'

Just then, the Muzak that was piped through the store stopped in mid-song. The PA system broadcast the ambient noise of a large number of people murmuring, snuffling, shifting in their chairs, and generally being alive. A suave voice Theo couldn't match up with any person he'd been introduced to yet said: 'Thank you for being patient. Please make sure that your cellphones are switched off. This is indeed a momentous occasion. It's not often in the history of publishing that a book can truly be said to have . . .' and so on and so on. Theo listened to the rhetoric as though it was apropos of something unconnected to him, something he'd mistakenly imagined he might wish to check out.

The Pixies man took a step closer to him, raising his sasquatch arm. Theo flinched, but the guy was only consulting a wristwatch.

'Showtime,' he said.

Acts

*L*et no one say our Saviour lacked
courage when the time came for him to
be crucified. For, to my sorrow, it has
been said. Simon of Capernaum, formerly the most
zealous of disciples, and now a whore-mongering
drunkard, declares to all who will listen that Jesus
died the same as any low wretch, the same as any
craven criminal, the same indeed as any farmyard
animal, without honour or nobility. How noble a
death would Simon die, in the same circumstances,
some might ask? But not I. Our Lord instructed
us to love our enemies. And it is an unfortunate
truth that Simon, who ought to have been a shining
light of our group, has become our enemy, and
would like nothing better than to see us snuffed
into darkness.

But no more of Simon. You asked me for an

account of our Saviour's final days, and instead I am wasting words on a man who spews cheap wine over his lap and consorts with whores. And not as our Lord consorted with whores, be it understood! I mean the behaviour of swine. But enough of Simon, and his vile aspersions on the courage of our Lord.

Cowardice in the face of grave injury is not a simple matter. The spirit can be brave while the body is weak. Or rather, the body acts without thought of bravery or weakness; it merely acts. When the soldiers seized upon the wrists of our dear Jesus to lay them flat against the crossbeam, and the man with the mallet bent near, our Lord cried out and pulled his arms to his sides, in the manner of an infant tickled by its mother. This was not cowardice. This is how the flesh behaves under such provocation.

I ask you, brothers and sisters, to imagine an iron spike brought near to the soft skin of your wrist, with the sure anticipation that in the next few moments, a mallet will drive that spike through your *flesh and the bones. Who among us would not flinch? Who among us would lie calm and say, Do what you must?*

In the garden where I met him first, our beloved Jesus gave himself to be sacrificed; that was his supreme act of courage. I witnessed the maker of the world deliver himself to be unmade. Simon asks again and again, Why was there no miracle? To which I say, How much more miraculous a miracle does Simon require, than that the Lord of all creation takes mortal form, and gives himself to be slaughtered? How strange it is that Simon was granted the privilege of daily companionship with Jesus, eating and walking and sitting with him, and receiving into his ears, that is to say into Simon's ears, all the wisdoms that Jesus spoke, and yet he understood nothing? Whereas I, who was in the presence of our Saviour only twice, and who possess not even two whole ears to hear with, have understood everything? But no more of Simon.

The soldiers placed their knees on our Lord's arms to keep them still, and tied him to the cross-

beam. Then they drove the spikes through the wrists of our dear Jesus. He cried out and two spouts of blood gushed up into the air. The soldiers worked quickly to finish their task, so that the wounds could soon be lifted high above the heart, and our Saviour should not be afforded the mercy of a death by bleeding. The crowd cheered as the cross settled upright into its hole. Forgive them, my friends. They did not hate Jesus. They did not hate any of the men being tortured that day.

Brothers and sisters, you have never witnessed a crucifixion; I pray that you never shall, for it is a terrible thing, arousing passions impossible to explain. All I will say is that there is a joy in seeing a difficult thing achieved. Two heavy beams of wood lie upon the ground, with a heavy man upon them (for Jesus, modest in stature though he was, was not small in girth); thus, when the lifting begins, also begins the doubt, whether such a weight might defeat the efforts of the lifters. Watching their exertions, one forgets the evil of the enterprise, and wishes only to add one's strength to the labour. The soldiers groan, *their faces turn red, the laden cross dips back towards the earth, and there is many a man in the crowd who leans his shoulder forward, as it were to share the burden. And many a woman also.*

Brothers and sisters, I am reminded that you asked me which of the disciples was present on that day. It is not an easy question to answer. Firstly, because a crucifixion lasts longer than a day; it is a torture rather than an execution, and there is rarely more than one victim finished by nightfall. The biggest crowd comes on the first day, but each day afterwards, a smaller crowd returns to see what progress has been made towards death. Secondly, when I came to Golgotha I was not yet acquainted with any of the disciples except Judas, and perhaps a couple of others I glimpsed in Gethsemane in poor light. I think I would remember the face of the man who cut off my ear. But I never saw that face again.

So, I can answer with certainty only in respect of the women. For they were already known to me, as the wives and daughters of elders of the temple.

Six or seven I saw there on Golgotha, huddled together for comfort. Rebekah and Abishag, whom you know from my other letters, and also the female kinfolk of other elders, including the daughter of Caiaphas himself.

How I despised those women, only a week before! Caiaphas and I discussed their dangerous foolishness, I recall, when first they fell under the spell of the uncouth prophet from Capernaum. We likened Jesus to a mad dog with a slavering mouth, afflicting the first woman with a contagion, which then spread from woman to woman, leaping from one empty head into the next. Or, say rather, one empty hole to the next, said Caiaphas, and I laughed like a jackass. How I squirmed with delight, at the honour of sharing a joke with the High Priest of the temple! And how much louder I would have laughed, if someone had dared prophesy to me that within a week I would be suffering the same contagion as those women! Oh, sweet contagion! May it spread from mouth to mouth and heart to heart, until the whole world is sick!

But to return to the story. The women of Jesus came to Golgotha, united in their sorrow. The daughter of Caiaphas was, as always, very beautiful, and her weeping made her no less so. Some women are ugly when weeping; others not. But I stray from the question; forgive me. As I have explained already, I cannot give an accurate account of the male disciples. There is no reason to doubt that Simon was there; we may mistrust everything about Simon, but not that. James and Andrew, as you know, became my friends in the weeks and months afterwards. They both swear that they were present, and it pains me to doubt them, for they love our Jesus with all their hearts; yet their memories of the particulars are at odds with what I witnessed with my eyes. All I will say is, If they were with us, they did not stay long.

Among the crucified that day was a man called Barnaby, whose onlookers were a large part of the crowd. He died quickly, because, as I heard, he was given poison by his brother. After the death of Barnaby, much of the crowd drifted back into town. If you have made a study, as I have, of the behaviour of people, you will know that they are like herds of cattle. A thing attracts one or two of their number, and others follow, and soon there is a multitude. Then somebody goes away, and one or two follow, then a dozen, and soon the multitude has vanished.

So it was on Golgotha. There was a jostling crowd to see our Saviour nailed up, but most of them had gone before the sun went down; and after Jesus was dead, the crowd dwindled to twenty or less. Our vigil on that hill, that is to say the vigil kept by the women and myself, waiting for our Lord to be taken off the cross, and watching the birds flying in circles around his head, was more lonely than I can tell. A few more disciples, if they had been there with us, might have allowed the time to pass more easily. Several other men were on that hill, waiting for their own brothers or fathers to be taken down, but, as I recall it, only Malchus and the women were waiting for Jesus. It is a difficult thing, to wait and not know when the waiting will end. Even so, I might have expected fishermen to be more patient in that respect.

But I see I have leapt to the end of the story, without telling the middle. Let us return, then, to the time when our dear Jesus was not yet dead. Forgive my leaping to and fro, brothers and sisters. I am a gossip by profession, not a historian. Also, my wretched state of health allows me to put pen to paper only once or twice a day, whereafter I must rest. If I were stronger, I might tell a better tale, a tale that flies from beginning to end with the sureness of an arrow. But what I have written I cannot unwrite.

So: the cross, with Jesus upon it, stood upright in its hole. It was the last cross to be erected that day. Six criminals were fixed in their places, with our Saviour sixth in the row. For the first hour, the spectacle on Golgotha was of the kind that holds the attention of a large crowd. The crucified men squirm and wriggle. They appear as unrestful sleepers, struggling in vain to find a position of comfort. Or they appear as men in the throes of carnal delight. But after a while, their movements become fewer, and each finds his own modest way of drawing the next breath. This is the juncture at which the crowds drift away, leaving only the dying man's family and friends.

Jesus cried out, Father, why have you forsaken me? and then hung in silence for a long time. His eyes were swollen and open, his mouth likewise. I waited. Other onlookers lost patience and turned their heads to watch elsewhere, but I kept my eyes unswervingly on Jesus. Finally his jaw began to turn, like the jaw of a cow. He uttered sounds I could not hear. I thought he might be speaking, or readying himself to speak, and I wished very much to hear the words. I walked closer, and, because the soldiers knew me, they allowed me to approach the cross, even to touch it. I gazed up at our beloved, in the shadow of his nakedness.

Please, somebody, please finish me, he cried. These were the last words that came from his mouth during his torment, although he spoke to me in other ways, which I will shortly describe.

His arms trembled fearsomely as he strove to pull himself higher, then he slipped down once more, and his innards opened of themselves. His urine fell on my face, and a foul liquid poured down the cross onto my hand. I heard the laughter of many in the crowd, and raucous advice in the Roman tongue. But I cared nothing for that. The urine of our Saviour burned on my forehead, burned through my skull into my soul. My eyes were blinded, and yet I could see more clearly than ever before.

I saw the world as it were from on high, higher than the highest mountain. The people far below, also the crowd assembled at Golgotha, seemed to me smaller than ants; and in their dispersing they were as raindrops on hot sand. The houses of the city were mere pebbles; the temple was a bauble in the dust.

And in my skull, the voice of Jesus spoke, saying, This world is a dream; its joys and sorrows are dreams. Rome is a dream, as is Jerusalem. Only I, Jesus, am. I am God, the maker and unmaker of worlds. I am the commander of angels, and yet

THE FIRE GOSPEL

*I see the lame one hurrying home when the sun sets,
and the widow tossing in her sleep.*

*Of what am I composed? I am composed of all
who believe in me. Together, we are both perfect and
mighty.*

And I say, Come, little raindrop: come into me.

Revelations

The first thing Theo was aware of when he regained consciousness was that he couldn't breathe. His arms were entirely numb; he wasn't even sure if he still had them. Maybe they'd been blown off? There was a stink of smoke in his clothing. Not cigarette smoke: bonfire-type smoke. His mouth was fused shut, as if the flesh was horribly burned, melted. He struggled to breathe through his nose, which was half blocked with crusted blood.

'He's suffocating, maybe,' said a voice. 'Shall we take the tape off now?'

'He'll holler,' said another voice.

'Nobody can hear him here,' said the first voice. Young men, both.

Strong fingers dug into Theo's cheek, found what they were feeling for, and ripped a rectangle of adhesive off his lips. He gasped in pain and relief.

Two faces loomed into his field of vision. One was a handsome Arab, with a glossy black kiss-curl and cupid lips; the other was a butt-ugly white guy of some sort, with no chin, thick glasses, a bulbous forehead and a few wisps of frizzy hair. A circus clown after five courses of chemotherapy.

'We're gonna make you sorry you ever lived,' the white guy promised, in a tone of voice that inspired belief.

The last thing Theo could remember before waking up in this strange apartment, bound hand and foot on a fat, fake-velour armchair, was taking questions from the audience at Pages bookstore. He had a clear mental picture of the assembled multitude, and no recollection of how he had got away from them.

His reading had been the usual set piece – Malchus's account of the crucifixion, edited to fit into the allotted twenty-five minutes – and his voice had held out OK. Then it was over and the assembled book lovers were doing their usual pluralistic thing: looking cool and unconcerned, looking distraught, weeping, shaking their heads, staring into their laps, glancing at their watches, serenely thumbing text messages into their cellphones, swaying in a trance of anguish, and so on.

In his journey across the United States, as sales of *The Fifth Gospel* had ignited beyond all forecasts, Theo had seen plenty of evidence of the book's power to devastate people, but he preferred to concentrate on evidence to the contrary. Just as an author of critically despised fiction may cling forever to a kind review in the *Sunday Times* in 1987 comparing him favourably to Thackeray, Theo clung to whatever he could, in his attempt to see *The Fifth Gospel* as an exhilarating historical discovery and a triumph of the translator's craft. Yeah, sure, there was widespread grief, but it was just one response among many; a minority response, maybe, even. What about that old man in Atlanta who said the book had reconciled him with his daughter? What about the guy in . . . in . . . forget the exact town, but the bookstore with the papier mâché bust of Shakespeare in its coffee shop? The guy there said that *The Fifth Gospel* was a breath of fresh air in the endlessly recycled atmosphere of Biblical scholarship. And then there was that young woman in Wilmington, a bit flaky admittedly, but friendly, who borrowed his signing pen to write her email address on her business card, so that they could continue their fascinating conversation about Aramaic in a 'more relaxed context', i.e. a context where there were no freaked-out people hanging around who looked as though they'd just had their souls ripped out.

Anyway, every town was different and you had to take each crowd on its own merits, and the New York crowd had been mixed, nothing out of the ordinary, no histrionics. Definitely cooler than some. The Q&A session, in Theo's opinion, was going fine, especially considering that he was out of his fucking mind with stress and 'erbil' medication at the time. Then a little guy in a golf shirt and checked pants said, 'Mr Griffin, have you heard the news from Kansas?'

'Kansas?' He considered making a *Wizard of Oz* joke, but had an instinct he shouldn't. 'What happened in Kansas?'

'A fifteen-year-old girl has just shot herself, like two hours ago. The cops found your book next to her on the bed.'

An uneasy murmur passed through the audience.

'That's . . . uh . . . terrible. Tragic. Awful,' said Theo. 'Is she dead?'

'Yes, Mr Griffin, she is dead.'

Theo said: 'I don't know what to say.'

'Well, the news reporter said that this girl read your book and lost all hope in life. What do you think about that, Mr Griffin?'

'Grippin,' interjected the bookstore employee who was MCing the event, in a polite but authoritative tone. 'Our guest this evening is Mr Theo *Grippin*.'

'I don't care what the hell his name is,' said the little guy, abruptly angry. 'What I wanna know is—'

And then . . . then what? A blinding light. A blow to the head. Darkness. And, after what seemed like several weeks of frustrated attempts to regain consciousness, a slow rematerialisation in this shabby apartment that smelled of old pizza and kebab juice. Even the armchair to which he was bound had that smell.

The apartment was eerily ill lit, with the ambience of a garage. Its contours were fuzzy. Actually, its contours weren't fuzzy: Theo's vision was. He had lost his glasses in the fracas at Pages.

'Where am I?' he called out. The two guys had moved to the other side of the room from where Theo was trussed up. They were conversing in soft voices, indecipherable to Theo because of the constant chatter issuing from a big old TV.

'Don't worry about that, pal,' retorted the white guy.

'You're not going anywhere,' added the Arab.

'They're expecting me in Boston,' said Theo. It was a dumb thing to say, obviously, but until he knew more about his abductors, everything he said was equally smart or dumb. He needed to engage them in dialogue.

'Your book tour is over, pal,' said the white guy.

'Live with it,' said the Arab.

Theo tugged at his bonds. He reasoned that if

he could tug and not achieve any result, he must still possess intact arms and hands, even though he couldn't feel them. They must have gone numb from the constriction or the unnatural angle. He was half seated, half slumped in the armchair, not upright enough to be properly supported but not low down enough to lie. His arms were draped over the padded arm rests, and he guessed that each of his wrists must be tethered to one of the back legs of the chair. His ankles were tied too, presumably to the front chair legs. He could hardly have been more uncomfortable if he'd been chained to a rock.

The chatter on the TV had metamorphosed from inane commercials to the news. A nasal female anchorperson repeated the afternoon's top stories. One of those was Theo's.

'Police are still searching for the two men who abducted controversial author Theo Grippin from Pages Bookstore in Penn Plaza, Manhattan at 9 p.m. last night. The kidnappers made their escape under cover of smoke from flare guns. Tragically, one of the flares set the store alight and three people lost their lives before the fire brigade arrived on the scene. Another ten people suffered burns and smoke inhalation; two of them are in a critical condition. Gloria McKinley reports from Manhattan.'

A different nasal female spoke. 'When Pages opened here in Penn Plaza last year, it dreamed of being the most popular bookstore in New York, with catchphrases like "All things to all readers" and "When is a chain not a chain?" As you can see behind me, that dream has turned to ashes. Mitch Merritt is the manager of Pages. Mitch, how do you feel?'

'Well, not too good, pretty bad in fact.' It was the Pixies guy. 'As you can see, our store is a mess. The fire and the water have destroyed a large proportion of what we had here, books and other stuff; the damage bill is gonna be in the region of . . . I can't even think about it. But of course those people who died . . . that's the real tragedy. We're in shock, all of us here at Pages, we're in shock.'

'Mitch, thank you.'

The report moved on to a précis of *The Fifth Gospel*, for the benefit of those viewers who weren't yet aware of what the anchorperson called its 'inflammatory' nature. Theo noted that she put the emphasis on the fourth syllable, vocalising 'oary' as a honking diph-thong, which reminded Theo of arguments he'd once had with Meredith about her annoying habit of saying 'interplanetoary' when she meant 'interplanetary', and 'cemetairy' when she meant 'cemetery'.

I'm going to die, he thought. And the last thing on my mind will be pedantic little linguistic hang-ups.

The TV news, having devoted more than three minutes to *The Fifth Gospel* and its tragic consequences, moved on to another calamity: Iraq. The female anchorperson deferred to the male anchorperson, whose name was Howard. He solemnly informed viewers (or, in Theo's case, listeners) that a partic-ular town near Baghdad had seen 'some of the fiercest fighting since the end of the war'. Statistics of various kinds were given, but Theo was still absorbing his own story, struggling to retrieve a phrase he'd barely taken in while busy obsessing over Meredith's pronunciation of 'cemetery'. It was something about police and urgent appeals for information. It was proof, in other words, that nobody had a clue where he might have been taken, or by whom, and that there was therefore zero chance of a lightning rescue.

Bad news, so much bad news on TV. But suddenly the network became aware of having transgressed the laws of entertainment, and offered penance in the form of a very brief report on a Japanese businessman who had bought John Lennon's bathrobe at auction for $350,000. 'John Lennon is revered here in Japan,' the businessman explained, in near-perfect English. 'This robe is full of history in so many ways. It was the robe he was wearing on the morning that his first wife Cynthia found him to have spent the night with Yoko. So it was not only next to John's skin, but . . . who knows what else?' To which the female anchor-person, as a way of bringing the pre-recorded segment to a cosy conclusion, added: 'Well, Howard, do you think maybe it's been washed a couple times since 1968?', allowing Howard to bounce back: 'I certainly hope so.'

And that was it as far as news went; sport would follow 'after the break'.

Theo had been leaning forward, straining to hear. He now tried to lean back, to rest his head against the well-stuffed fabric of the armchair. But the way he'd been tied up didn't really permit it. Abruptly, he was energised by a vehement kind of claustrophobia, a deep conviction that he couldn't endure this any longer, and he lunged against his constraints. For the duration of his lunge, perhaps two seconds, he was able to imagine himself snapping the legs of the armchair – cheap, spindly legs weakened by woodworm, perhaps – and jumping to his feet with a mighty gasp of relief, Prometheus unbound. It was a wonderful vision. But nothing more.

'Campbell signed a two-year contract in the offseason,' chattered the TV, 'that could be worth up to 10.5 million dollars. He's expected to split time with last year's starter Duke LaMont as the Giants try to improve a running game that averaged 4.3 yards per carry . . .'

'Excuse me?' called Theo weakly. 'Excuse me?'

'Whaddaya want, minion of Satan?' the white guy snapped back.

For a few seconds, Theo had difficulty thinking of a reply. He wasn't used to being called 'minion of Satan', except in Amazon reviews.

'I'm very thirsty,' he said, and it was true. His voice was hoarse and it hurt him to speak. 'May I have a drink of water?'

'I wouldn't recommend it, pal.'

'Why not?'

'What goes in must come out. Don't want to get yourself all wet, do you?'

Theo considered this for a moment. 'I'll take the risk,' he croaked. 'My throat feels like it's lined with hot ashes.'

'That's too bad.'

The two strange men resumed their conversation. However, a new note of tension had entered it, and after a minute or two, the Arab lost his patience and spoke a lot louder.

'If he's gonna speak for the broadcast, he will need a voice. A voice that sounds like him, like he should sound! If he sounds weird, people will say the tape is a fake.'

A couple of minutes passed. Then a dark hand hovered near Theo's face, holding a can of Pepsi.

'Open up, man.'

Theo pursed his lips and allowed the Arab to trickle the cola into his parched mouth. It stung like blazes. Water would have been better. Maybe this was part of the torture. Or maybe this was the kind of bachelor apartment where there were never any clean cups or glasses to put water in.

'Thank you,' said Theo. Spilled cola was fizzing on his stubbly chin, and in the fibres of his shirt. His throat felt better, though.

'You're welcome,' said the Arab instinctively, and retreated from view.

They made him wait, these guys: oh, how they made him wait. The Arab walked past him several times, fetching food and drink for his friend, who remained installed in front of the TV. The Arab was a smallish young man, dressed in American casuals. His skin contrasted nicely with the blue of his shirt. Theo considered calling out *Hey, nice shirt!* or something similar, in case it made any difference. But he was inhibited by how artificial that would sound. Despite having been abducted and tied to an armchair by two desperate characters, possibly psychotics who were planning to murder him, he was too embarrassed to utter compliments that were transparent attempts to ingratiate himself. Instead, he called 'Excuse me?' and 'Hello?' every so often, suspecting that this was precisely the wussy-ass course of action pursued by doomed hostages just before they received a bullet through the brain.

Over on the other side of the room, the TV news had given way to a rerun of a comedy show from the mid-1990s.

'Are you watching this?' said the Arab after a while.

There was no audible reply from the white guy, but he must have indicated No, because the Arab said, 'Then why don't we turn it off?'

'There could be a newsflash.'

'A newsflash about what? About us?'

'Maybe.'

'Forget it, man. What you think they're gonna say? They found out where we live and the cops are on their way? If that happens, for sure there won't be a tip-off on the TV.'

'But I don't *wanna* be Switzerland!' whined a voice on the TV, followed by a burst of what sounded like a flock of ravenous seagulls: the laughter track of a typical American sitcom.

'Jews, man!' said the Arab testily. 'Do we have to watch these Jews? Talking about nothing, laughing about nothing; empty lives, man! And this Seinfeld guy, I read about him, he's the richest man in show business, he's got his own aircraft hangar where he puts all these Porsches he never drives, because he's got a chauffeur. It's everything that's wrong with this country, man! You hear those people laughing their heads off? They're laughing at *us*, man.'

'Calm down, Nuri. You're being paranoid.'

'Me, paranoid? When *you're* sitting there in front of a Jew comedy rerun waiting for a newsflash about *you*? There won't be a newsflash, man, until we've done the tape. *Then* there'll be a newsflash.'

Theo hung his head onto his chest, inhaling the aromas of smoke-impregnated shirt and sugary cola. *The tape*. This was the second reference they'd made to *the tape*. The tape of his execution? Theo tried to imagine himself as the sort of person who survives a deadly ordeal and writes a book about it afterwards. *I made a mental list of everything I'd learned so far. (1) – One of my captors was called Nuri. (2) – I was expected to speak on a tape, for the purpose of an as-yet-unspecified broadcast. All of a sudden, in a flash of inspiration, I realised the key to my escape.* Theo closed his eyes, the better to see the flash of inspiration. He saw only darkness.

A warm hand slapped him gently on the cheek. He opened his eyes. Once more, the two strange faces loomed before him. The Arab's expression betrayed more stress than before, his lush black eyebrows almost knitted together.

The white guy looked slightly more relaxed, or perhaps just more spaced out. 'This *had* to happen, you *know* that, don't you?' he drawled, in an oddly sensuous tone. 'We're just playing our parts.'

'I'm not sure what you mean,' said Theo, 'but if I've upset you personally in any way . . .'

'You will atone,' the white guy assured him. 'You will atone.'

Several hours later, Theo had learned all he wanted to, and more, about the two men's motives in kidnapping him.

The short answer was that they felt that *The Fifth Gospel* was interfering with the natural function of the socio-political landscape, and they wanted him to recite a prepared speech on video camera, which they would then distribute to the media.

The long answer was, in Theo's estimation, two hours longer than it needed to be. A transcript of it would have filled a book, and that book, if a publisher had taken it on, would have cried out for a clearheaded editor. But the story as told by Nuri and his unnamed white associate would never be subjected to an editor's scrutiny; it was inscribed on these guys' mushy brains, in microscopic, incoherent, half-dissolved handwriting, an intricate labour of love that only they could decode.

Nuri's beef with *The Fifth Gospel*, as far as Theo could make sense of it, was that it was a tool of Zionism. Malchus's story demoralised Christians and made them doubt the Godhood of Christ. This lent credence to the Jews' contention that Jesus was not the Messiah, and encouraged those Christians who were not quite ready to ditch the Bible altogether to regard the New Testament as a spurious addendum to the Old. Already in some states of America and, for some unknown reason, in Romania and Hungary, there was an upsurge of brand new Christian sects, who believed that the Christ was yet to come and could be identified by rigorous study of the Old Testament. There'd been TV footage of converts demonstrating in Balkan towns, holding Bibles aloft and ceremonially slicing off the New Testament with a sharp knife through the spine. Nuri couldn't care less about these sects, and thought they were crazy. He was a Muslim. What he cared about was that these sects were a symptom of Christianity in disarray and a shift towards the Torah as the supreme religious authority in the West. Inevitably, this would strengthen the self-confidence of the Jews, help their recruitment, and lead to a gross expansion of Zionism, which in turn would add to the misery of the Palestinians. The insidious progress towards Zionist supremacy would be twofold: key members of the American administration would defect from Christianity and convert to the Jewish faith, and their policies would meet with less opposition than usual because thousands of voters would be embracing Judaism likewise. Thus, the memoirs of Malchus would, in time, prove directly responsible for a total genocide of Muslims in Palestine.

The white guy's theory, comparatively speaking, was a little bizarre. It lacked the political acuity of Nuri's analysis, and its logical structure was less sound. Also, it was heavy on the polysyllables, which, given that the guy had the physical appearance and accent Theo might expect of a trolley collector at Wal-Mart, gave his whole spiel an air of incongruity. Might the guy merely be parroting the contents of a book? If so, his memorising and regurgitating skills were impressive.

The gist of the argument, if the word 'gist' could be applied to a vat of refried beans, was that Jesus had never existed in corporeal form, but was a hologram, or pan-focal dwell-point, brought into being by God. The so-called disciples were magickal adepts, biospiritual channels, whose sacred task was to transform input from God into hologrammatical output. In selected locations – the seashore at Galilee, the wedding at Cana, Golgotha and so on – they would stand in special positions and, through mutual focus, create a synchronised manifestation of a living pseudoperson, i.e. Jesus. The historical impact of these manifestations was part of an ongoing project on God's part to improve the human race; an event like the crucifixion was intended as an evolutionary trigger, propelling chosen individuals to become prototypes for a superior form of Homo sapiens. Trouble was, Satan was also a player in this game, and his agenda was to prevent these evolutionary advances, and keep mankind in a state of brutish ignorance, so that, instead of embracing pure living and sexual abstinence, they fell into the clutches of sin, and ended up in Hell.

At this point, the white guy had paused in his explanation, and fetched some sort of shrinkwrapped muffin and a Pepsi, because he'd been talking for a long time without food or drink, and besides his throat was a little raw too, having inhaled the same smoke as Theo.

'So . . . uh . . . where do I come in?' Theo ventured to ask.

'Satan is the Prince of Lies,' said the white guy, munching on his muffin. 'And Malchus was one of his channels. Malchus was chosen by Satan to undermine the power of the crucifixion. The adepts were onto him, but he outsmarted them, and hid the scrolls in a pregnant belly. Because God does not look into pregnant bellies. It's part of the deal with Gaia.'

'I didn't know that,' said Theo.

'Not many people know that. But it explains why there's birth defects, miscarriages, stuff like that. God could theoretically look in there and fix it, but, like I said, that was the deal.'

'It sounds like a bad deal.'

The white guy shrugged. 'The universe needs to keep in harmony with the female principle,' he said, without much enthusiasm.

'So, uh . . . how do I fit into the scheme of things?'

'You were fooled by Satan's lies, and you've translated them, and you've poisoned the world with your book. But the media is open to antidotes as well as poisons. So, we're gonna sit you in front of a video camera, and you're gonna undo the damage you've done.'

'By explaining to the viewers what you've just explained to me?'

The white guy laughed out loud, revealing large, irregular teeth. 'Are you kidding? Nobody would believe that. The truth is too complicated and most people's minds can't handle it. They can only handle a simple story. A real simple story.' He reached into his shirt pocket and pulled out a folded square of paper. 'So . . . we've written one for you.'

Interlude: A Prophecy

Less than a day after the end of this book, the following will come to pass:

Meredith and her boyfriend will be cooling off after making love, allowing the sweat to evaporate from their naked bodies. Meredith will take a swig from the Perrier bottle next to the bed. The water has gone lukewarm in the broiling heat of Paris.

The TV is still on and, now that their lovemaking is over, it seems unnecessarily loud. Meredith wishes that it hadn't been necessary to switch it on in the first place, but Robert is in the habit of making extraordinary noises when approaching orgasm, and each morning she has to face the other guests in the breakfast room.

It has gone on long enough, this holiday. She's tired of the heat, the shopping for clothes she isn't French enough to fit into, Robert's bellowing in bed, his useless info about camera apertures and narrow escapes from predators. She is even a little tired of her own orgasms. They're like an addiction to blintzes or something; she keeps having more, when she's only just had the last, and no sooner does she tell herself that she'll never need another one in her whole life, than she's being jigged on the bed with her knees against Robert's ears and her toes banging against the polished brass of the bedhead.

She pours a little of the Perrier into her palm, and splashes it on her forehead. The TV has progressed to the news. A French voice is saying something about *Le Cinquième Évangile*. Then a video of Theo comes on. He is sitting in an armchair, in a casual pose, wearing exactly the sort of horrible shirt he always threatened to buy when he was with her. He looks OK despite it. He isn't wearing his glasses, and looks better for that, too.

'I want to apologise,' he says, and a simultaneous translation flashes across the bottom of the screen: *Je veux demander pardon.*

Lamentations

Theo smiled sheepishly into the beam of light trained on him from a desk lamp. The white guy allowed the second-last cue card to fall to the floor and held aloft the final portion of text. As on the previous sheets, the words were printed giant sized and correctly spelled. At the very bottom, handwritten in red pen, was the message WAVE AT THE CAMERA.

'And . . . and that's all I have to say, really,' said Theo. 'When I made this stuff up, I never thought it would lead to anyone getting hurt. I just wanted to get rich and I figured that fooling people was a good way to do it. It was a lousy thing to do and I don't expect you to forgive me. But please forgive me anyway. And . . . uh . . . put my book in the trash can where it belongs, OK?'

He waved awkwardly at the camera, as per instruction. Nuri switched off the taping mechanism. Silence descended. The shotgun lay across the white guy's knees, pointed at Theo, just as before. Theo was naturally rather curious whether, now that the video-tape was in the bag, he would be allowed to live.

'How did I do?' he asked, his voice catching.

'You did great,' said the white guy, without any perceptible emotion.

'Well, I did my best,' said Theo, fresh sweat breaking out on his forehead. This time, Nuri did not lean over with a white cloth and dab it up. 'The little hesitations . . . I don't know if you noticed, but they were deliberate, actually. I thought they made it sound more natural. Like I was thinking on my feet, you know?'

'It's not a problem,' said the white guy.

Theo sat back gingerly in the armchair, folding his hands in his lap, in slow motion. Maybe if he didn't make any conspicuous movements with his arms, these guys would let him stay untied for a while longer. It was wonderful to have his arms free. Even if he couldn't put them to any particular use, it was still a divine relief not to have ten yards of packing twine digging into his wrists.

'Tie him up again,' said the white guy.

Nuri and the white guy sat on the couch with the TV on, and played back the videotape to check it was OK. A babel of voices ensued. On TV, a chef explained the difference between frying and searing, while Theo's confession was fast-forwarded and rewound repeatedly, while Nuri and the white guy discussed the merits and demerits of the recording.

'Cut out the pauses,' the white guy decided. 'They're useless. Dead air.'

'The TV people will cut them out, if they need to,' said Nuri. 'They've got equipment.'

'We shouldn't tempt them. They might cut out more than they should. If we give 'em something they can broadcast just the way it comes, they might leave it alone.'

'They'll leave it alone anyway,' said Nuri. 'This is dynamite news, man. This is what they call a *scoop.*' He pronounced this last word with a typically Arabic inflection, making it sound like a central tenet of Islam.

'And just as that li'l ol' steak is starting to yell "ouch",' said the TV chef, 'you pull him out of the pan, see?'

'Cut out the pauses,' said the white guy.

'Then you drown him in a generous slug of this wine, like so . . .'

'. . . chose it because there's such a huge market for books about Jesus,' recited the voice of Theo Grippin. 'I mean . . . uh . . . look at *The Da Vinci Co* . . . out Jesus. I mean . . . uh . . . Jesus. I . . .'

'This is difficult,' complained Nuri. 'If I make a mistake, we have to record the whole thing again.'

'No sweat. We got him right there.'

'I would find this a lot easier if the TV was off, man.'

'Just cut out a few pauses, Nuri; it's a camcorder, it's not rocket science.'

'Meanwhile, the eggplants are sautéing along nicely there . . .'

'There is no silence ever anymore in our place,' lamented Nuri. 'We used to enjoy the silence.'

'There'll be plenty of silence soon enough.'

'How about *now*, man?'

'The news is on in five minutes.'

And so it went on. Theo Grippin's voice hiccupped its way backwards and forwards through his confession, repeating phrases like 'faked the scrolls' and 'my greed' over and over. '*Et voilà!*' exclaimed the TV chef. 'That's French for dee-*lish*.'

Theo's arms were going numb again. He was bound slightly less uncomfortably than before, because last time he'd been slumped unconscious while the men were tying him up, whereas this time he'd tried to position himself in such a way that only his arms and ankles were pulled askew. He'd also been permitted, just before his video perform- ance, to take a piss in a jumbo soft drink cup, so the pressure on his bladder had eased. Inconveniently, however, he now felt a growing fullness in his bowels, despite not having eaten for a day and a half.

If he survived to write a book about his captivity, he might have to go easy on the uro-gastro- intestinal stuff, if he didn't want to come across like Malchus.

'The search continues,' said the news anchor-woman, 'for the two men who abducted controversial author Theo Grippin from Pages Bookstore in Penn Plaza, Manhattan on Tuesday. The kidnappers set off flares which set the store alight, causing the deaths of three people. One other person seriously injured in the blaze has died this morning in Bellevue Hospital. He was Martin F. Salati, a literary agent. In a separate incident in Placitas, Santa Fe, a man was killed during a public bonfire of copies of Grippin's book *The Fifth Gospel*. The man poured gasoline on the books, unaware that an aborted attempt had already been made to light the fire. The stream of gasoline ignited and exploded the gasoline can, engulfing the man in flames. Santa Fe City councillor John Delacruz had this to say:'

'In my opinion, this book should not be called *The Fifth Gospel*, they should call it *The Fire Gospel*. I appeal to all citizens ever'where to please calm down. If you got to read this thing, then read it, but don't risk your life over it. Remember, it's only a book.'

Damn right! Theo wanted to yell across the room,

but he held his tongue. Abruptly, the TV switched off and the apartment was quiet at last.

'What you do that for?' said the white guy.

'We've seen enough.'

'Have it your way, Nuri.'

There was a pause. A screwtop was twisted off a bottle, releasing a sharp hiss.

'We shouldn't have burned those people down,' said Nuri.

'We didn't burn anybody down. There was a fire, an accidental fire.'

'We shouldn't have burned those people down,' Nuri repeated. His tone was not particularly anguished or argumentative, more like the deep, long-digested regret felt by someone who sold off all his treasured childhood possessions years ago and wishes he had them back.

'They were supporters of Grippin,' said the white guy. 'They came to sit at his feet.'

'There were chairs,' Nuri pointed out.

'I mean they came to admire him. To worship him, almost! You heard them applaud, Nuri. They would've asked for autographs if they'd got the chance.'

'We never discussed burning them down. The flares were only to make smoke.'

'It's regrettable. Those folks died sooner than they shoulda, maybe. But they're gonna be burning in Hell *forever*, Nuri. That's a lot longer than a half hour in a bookstore.'

This seemed to satisfy the Arab. He resumed editing Theo's confession.

'And . . . and that's all I have to say, really,' said the voice of Grippin. 'And . . . and that . . . And that's all . . .'

While Nuri was out delivering the videotape to the nearest TV station, the white guy stayed at home. Theo had hoped it would be the other way round, i.e. white guy out and Nuri in, because he suspected he might be able to communicate on a more . . . what was the word? . . . *humane* level with Nuri. But evidently the white guy suspected the same thing.

Theo laid his head on the arm of the armchair,

trying to find a position of less discomfort. The implications of what he had just done were sinking in. Millions of people who'd merely resented him before would now hate him with a passion. Christians and non-Christians alike would spit on him in the street. And for what?

Good question, good question. A hundred times in the last few weeks he'd been asked by interviewers what his motives were in unleashing *The Fifth Gospel* on the world, and he'd given various bullshit answers. But underneath it all, he'd nourished a secret ambition, an ambition he'd scarcely admitted to himself. He was not, by nature, an altruistic guy; he had never had much time for idealists. But when it came to *The Fifth Gospel*, he had been forced under relentless probing to uncover the illicit idealism hidden inside him: he wanted to help the human race evolve. He wanted to give them the means to break their addiction to religion, to stop worshipping the dead and start solving the problems of the living. Malchus's innocently devastating memoir would blow away two thousand years of mumbo-jumbo and light the flame of reason, and millions of spiritual cripples would throw away their crutches and take responsibility for themselves.

Go easy on the hubris, lover, Jennifer would no doubt have said.

Anyway, that hope was erased. Soon, the cringing confession of Theo Grippin would be broadcast; every country where the book had been sold would run the footage of literature's most despicable con man. Forget the flame of reason; the only flame the world would want to light would be under Theo Grippin.

Then again, would people really believe his confession was genuine? Could anyone be that credulous? Probably. If there was one thing the Pandora's box of Amazon customer reviews had taught him, it was that there was no fiction so outrageously, laughably, arrogantly false that somebody somewhere wasn't moved to tears by its truth. Maybe he should have planted some clues in his performance, odd gestures or rhythmic eye-blinks to convey coded meanings that could be extracted by detectives. Although, given that he had zero idea of this apartment's location or the identities of his kidnappers, it was difficult to imagine what hidden meanings he could've attempted.

How long till the videotape was delivered and Nuri returned? The Arab had promised not to be long: how long was not long? Even assuming that the apartment was somewhere in New York City – which was by no means certain – the whereabouts of the nearest TV studio were equally unguessable. Moreover, there was no clock within Theo's range of vision, and his wristwatch was useless on his swollen wrist, pinioned behind the armchair in a tangle of twine. Despite all these indications that there was no point trying to predict when the Arab would come back, Theo felt he should try to keep track of time. It was the sort of thing that survivors did, people who kept their head in a crisis. He considered counting to sixty over and over, logging the minutes with a click of his parched tongue.

'Virgin Galactic plans to fly five hundred passengers a year into space, at a cost of 200,000 dollars each . . .'

The TV was on again, which in theory ought to

have made it easier to calculate the passing minutes and hours, but in fact made it harder. A swirling vortex of inane infotainment emanated from the box, frenetic and casual, tedious and tantalising, always on the edge of a climax, never getting started, permanently stalled and in a hurry, promising to return in a moment.

It wouldn't be so bad if he could see the images instead of merely hearing the voices. Tied to the chair, he could see only what was right in front of him, which was a bookcase filled with paperbacks whose gaudy spines he couldn't decipher without glasses. If he twisted his head, he could catch a glimpse of the closed door to the bathroom.

'Controversial rapper Bad Boy Ammo is suing the Toyota motor company for using his image without permission. He claims that an advertisement depicting a cartoon street punk attempting to steal the hubcaps from a Toyota Omega is modelled on his likeness. Bad Boy's lawyers have denounced the ad as "vile" and "tasteless" and have filed a lawsuit for 1.5 million dollars in damages.'

Theo dug his head hard into the upholstery of the

chair and tried to quell another surge of claustrophobia. If only he could be not so thoroughly trussed
up; if only there could be some slack. If only they
would agree to tie him to a heavy object by one wrist,
or maybe by his neck, doggy-leash style. He would
be so grateful, he wouldn't even attempt to escape.
If only he could get the white guy to believe that.
Then he could breathe. And maybe escape.

He tried to think of something else. A man called
Bad Boy was seeking $1.5 million damages for the
pain of being accused, albeit in cartoon form, of
bad behaviour. An American sitcom writer had
earned multimillions from a show about nothing.
A football player had agreed to kick a ball around
a field for $10.5 million. And what had he, Theo,
got in return for *The Fifth Gospel*? A lousy $250,000
advance. Plus some hot sex. Plus maybe a few million
dollars in royalties, if he survived to spend them.

Hold on a second: why was he thinking such
materialistic thoughts? Weren't people faced with
death supposed to have noble epiphanies? Weren't
they supposed to transcend petty obsessions and gain

insight into essential truths? What was the deal here? Why was he even *capable* of resenting the fortunes of footballers and stand-up comedians, when his brain might be hosting its final few thoughts before total extinction? Why was there room for wondering where the book-burners in Santa Fe had procured their sacrificial copies of *The Fifth Gospel* (a sale is a sale, right?) but no room for transformative wisdom?

Or was that the real lesson here? That human consciousness was too flighty and distractible to submit to the neat discipline of enlightenment, even under pressure of death? When Robert F. Kennedy lay bleeding to death on the pantry floor of the Ambassador Hotel, did he review his contributions to the welfare of America's poor and disenfranchised, and gain peace in the knowledge that he'd done what he could – or was he noting speckles of unhygienic grime on the ceiling fan? Were Martin Luther King's last thoughts about the lousy room service he had suffered that morning? Did Abraham Lincoln, when sprawled in the balcony of Ford's Theater with a bullet in his brain, feel profound gratitude that he'd been permitted to donate the words 'all men are created equal' to human history, or did he spend his final few seconds of sentience puzzling over the precise meaning of 'you sockdologizing old man-trap', the farcical punchline he'd just heard uttered onstage?

And Jesus? What about Jesus? He hung dying for hours, maybe days; he'd had ample opportunity to conceive all manner of epiphanies and perfect, poignant dying words. Instead, if Malchus was to be believed, he probably spent the whole time focusing on how extremely exquisitely fucking painful it was to have a spike stuck through your wrist. Or maybe he was really, really worried about shitting himself with his mother watching.

Ah, yes: shitting oneself. There was a good reason why Theo might be reminded of that aspect of human potential just now: he was brewing a bout of diarrhoea. It stewed in his lower bowel, sending knife-sharp pains through him. For the last hour already, he'd been playing the dangerous game of allowing his anus to open just slightly and momentarily, every ten minutes or so, to release a small amount of toxic gas. It was inconceivable that the white guy couldn't smell what was going on, but he continued to sit silent in front of the TV.

'A hand-tooled genuine cowhide leather sheath is included in the price if you order now!'

Even in his distress, Theo couldn't help reflecting upon the mysteries of coincidence: to hear the same TV advertisement in his kidnappers' apartment as he'd happened to hear in a Los Angeles hotel. It was this sort of thing that made people perceive all experience as connected, he was sure. It was this sort of thing that appealed to the mentally ill.

'So,' he said, trying to sound casual while raising his voice sufficiently to project it to the other side of the room. 'How did you guys meet?'

There was no reply. Theo was scared to repeat the question in case it led to another strip of adhesive tape being stuck over his mouth.

The TV started singing, a glee club kind of choir, extolling the virtues of toothpaste. It was a post-ironic commercial, nostalgically yearning for the Eisenhower-era innocence that had been referenced satirically in 1990s commercials until the satire itself got old. *We used to make fun of those clean-cut Doris Day types singing jingles in praise of margarine*, the new subtext was suggesting, *but now we know that those people inhabited a simpler age, a lost paradise.*

'Filth,' said the white guy. He seemed to be addressing no one in particular, certainly not Theo. 'Human garbage. Scum, scum, scum, scum.'

'Excuse me,' called Theo. 'I really, *really* need to go to the bathroom.'

There was a couple of seconds' pause, then an almighty crash as a table laden with plates and cups was kicked over. Theo gasped in surprise as the white guy's face abruptly hovered inches from his own. It was a terrifying visage: beaded with oily drops of sweat, bug-eyed with fury, grey skinned, panting breath that was sweet with medication.

'You gonna sit tight,' he hissed. 'You gonna sit tight until this is over.'

'Until what's over?'

The white guy's eyes seemed to effervesce with pain. He was almost nose to nose with Theo.

'*All* this,' he choked, and waved his arm wildly behind him, sweeping across the whole room, the whole world.

And His Chains Fell Off
From His Hands

In the space of an hour, or maybe two hours, or possibly three, a thousand and one lives were chronicled for several seconds each. Celebrities came to prominence, achieved their dreams, went into rehab, and died. Sportsmen were bought and sold. Musicians were permitted to play a snatch of song before being swept aside by commercials. Politicians explained why they were right, and actors enthused about their latest movies, and a woman from Bermuda showed off her cat, which weighed forty-eight pounds. Theo couldn't see the cat, of course, but a voice told him that it was approximately as heavy as a six-year-old boy, which conjured up quite a vivid picture. Other voices told him about a coachload of schoolchildren in Lahore who'd fallen into a ravine, the terrible danger posed to the universe by the Lizard Men of Ultima 6, his very last chance to get a genuine replica Dupont lighter for only $99.99, his unrepeatable final opportunity to get a genuine non-replica Hermès keychain for $49, and how Chantal was determined to go through with the wedding even though Jo-Jo had given her positive proof that Brad seduced her own mother.

Theo thought he might be slipping into delirium. The door kept opening and then a few more minutes would go by and it would open again, because it hadn't opened before, he'd only wished it had, and then a few more minutes would go by, and finally the door would open, for *real* this time, and then a few more minutes would go by, during which the door was evidently still closed, and all the while, voices on the TV were laughing and hissing and gibbering.

Finally the door opened.

'What's that smell?' said the Arab, as soon as he'd stepped into the apartment.

'Never mind the smell,' said the white guy. 'What happened with the tape?'

Nuri closed the door behind him, removed his coat with a rustle of nylon. 'I delivered it to the TV station.'

'What took you so long?'

'It's two bus rides. And I had to wait for the right moment.'

'Are you sure they got it?'

'As sure as I can be.'

'Did you actually see somebody unwrap it?'

'Of course I didn't. Relax, man. This, they are not gonna ignore. It will be all over America by tomorrow. Tonight, maybe, even!' He sounded boyishly pleased. He was waiting for his pat on the back.

'I've been going out of my *mind* here, Nuri,' said the white guy, his voice made even uglier by an asthmatic wheeze. 'Thinking you'd screwed up.'

'You gotta trust me, man! What's got into you? Whatever happened to, you know: "Two men, two faiths, one mission"?'

'Sit down, Nuri,' said the white guy wearily. 'We gotta watch TV until that thing comes on.'

But Nuri was not so easily bidden. 'Oh, come on, man. You *know* how I feel about television. Jewish sitcoms, Jewish news, soap operas . . . It's bad for the brain, man! We used to talk all the time. Now we don't talk.'

'Sure we talk.'

'Not like before.'

'Well, the situation has changed.'

There was a pause.

'What are we going to do with Grippin, man?' said Nuri.

'Nothing.'

'We can't do nothing.'

'Sure we can do nothing.'

'You said we would drive him upstate and let him go in the woods.'

'That was assuming we had a car. We had to dump the car. So what do you think we're gonna do now, carry him fifty miles on our backs? Take him for a trip in the bus? "*Oh, and one ticket for our pal with the blindfold and the adhesive strip on his mouth*"?'

'You told me the woods.'

'Forget the woods. It was a nice idea. Nice ideas get left behind sometimes. We got to adjust to reality.'

Another pause.

'So,' said Nuri. 'You gonna shoot the guy? Is that what you're gonna do?'

'Relax, pal. We just let nature take its course.'

'Nature? What you mean nature?'

'I mean, don't give him any more fuckin' *Pepsi*,' snapped the white guy. 'Don't give him any more *nothing*.'

'Don't curse, man. We don't curse, remember? We honour God with our mouth, remember?'

'Yeah, yeah . . . whatever.'

'I'm not gonna take this,' said Nuri.

'Yes, you are,' said the white guy, sounding sullen and exhausted and rather petulant. 'You are gonna sit down here next to me and we are gonna watch the TV until the news comes on.'

'I am not gonna sit here for two weeks or whatever while a guy dies of thirsting and starving in our armchair. Have you gone crazy?'

The white guy leapt up, yelling: 'You want a quick solution, pal? You wanna go straight to the end?'

A scuffle erupted: grunting and stumbling and

cries of exertion. Theo imagined the two men locked in titanic combat; he had a hopeful vision of them in a wrestling clinch over the shotgun and it firing accidentally and the white guy sprawling on the floor, dead. Instead, a moment later, the white guy and his shotgun jumped right in front of him, the barrel aimed straight at Theo's face.

How disappointing, was all he had time to think before the big bang.

The bullet had blown him through space, way past the sky, way past the moon. He was adrift in the solar system, a million miles above the earth. He was still tied to the armchair, and he and it spun slowly in the airless blackness, tempting him with the illusion that the stars and planets were revolving around him. He knew this was not so. He was a small puppet of meat from Canada, with a hole blasted in it, twirling in the void like any other particle of debris.

'We are dust,' Malchus had said, in the conclusion of his Gospel. 'But we are dust with a mission.

We carry within us the seeds of our Saviour, which will blossom in those who come after us.'

Damn, thought Theo. *I should have had children.*

'I'm sorry, man,' said Nuri. 'I'm sorry.'

Theo's universe stopped revolving, and coalesced into a young Arab who was kneeling at his feet.

Theo squirmed in the chair, gasping for breath, dizzy with the adrenalin of having been dropped back into his body from a height of a million miles. Nuri grunted with effort as he untied the bonds around Theo's ankles.

'You better go to a hospital,' the Arab said.

Theo's newly freed hands raced over the surface of his body, stroking his face, his neck, his chest, his stomach, in search of holes. His clothing was covered in charred fragments of polyurethane foam. His palm came to rest on his right side, just under his ribcage, where he felt bubbling wetness and raw pain.

'Don't mess with it, man,' advised Nuri.

'Oh my God,' moaned Theo. 'I'm going to die.'

'You're not going to die,' said Nuri. 'It's not deep. It's . . . uh . . .' He flapped his plump fingers delicately, to indicate a lightness of touch.

'Superficial?'

'That's the word,' said Nuri. And he indicated a large hole in the chair, where the bullet had wrought most of its harm.

The apartment was eerily quiet. The TV had stopped chattering. The window blinds, which had been constantly closed since Theo's arrival, had been raised, revealing a cloudy late-afternoon sky.

'What happened?' said Theo. 'Where's . . . uh . . . your friend?'

'He tried to shoot you. But I turned away the gun.'

'Is he dead?'

'No, he's . . . sleeping.' Nuri glanced over to the other side of the room, then down at his own soft hands.

'You knocked him out?'

Nuri seemed a little embarrassed at this allusion to his physical prowess. 'He's not very strong. He's . . . he's sick, man. His bones, his whole system, the news is not good. He takes maybe ten, fifteen pills a day.'

Theo couldn't think how to respond to this.

'You saved my life,' he said at last. 'Thank you.'

Nuri appeared not to have heard. He had other things he was chewing through, things that were more urgently in need of articulation. 'You shouldn't judge him, man,' he said, with the utmost sincerity. 'He wasn't always like this. He used to be . . .' Nuri's luxurious brown eyes misted over, as he gazed back into the history of his relationship with the white guy. 'More or less exactly like a Muslim,' he concluded.

Theo sat upright. His side throbbed, and he was aware that his bowels had opened.

'What happens next?' he asked Nuri.

Nuri shrugged, as if there was no point consulting him. 'I don't know. You're free to go, I guess. I never wanted any of this trouble. I just wanted to put a stop to your book and that's what I did. Mission accomplished. You can call the police, I don't care. I'm not afraid of jail. I'm not afraid of anything.'

Theo tried to stand, fell back into the armchair. More fragments of stuffing puffed out of the gunshot hole. Nuri took hold of Theo's wrist and hauled him upright.

'I won't tell anyone, I promise,' said Theo. Blood pattered onto the carpet at his feet. He would have to get hold of a bandage of some sort, if that wasn't pushing his luck.

Nuri was unimpressed with Theo's promise. 'I know you'll tell everybody who'll listen that your confession was a fake,' he said. 'But it won't matter. The story is out there. Once a story is out there, you can never take it back. That's the way it is.'

'I meant, I won't tell anyone about *you*. I'll say I couldn't see who kidnapped me; they wore masks the whole time. And . . . and I'll say they drove me to the woods.'

Nuri smiled shyly.

Theo got ready as fast as he could, given the handicaps of a grisly, freely bleeding gunshot wound, dehydration and shit-filled pants. His fear was that while he was in the bathroom, squeezing brown soup out of a sponge, the white guy would wake up and shoot him again. Six weeks later, the cops would break into the place and find the skeletal corpse of Theo Grippin with its head blown clean off, all because Theo had spent too long fastidiously sponging his testicles. But the white guy didn't wake up. He remained unconscious on the couch, tucked up in a blanket. His mouth hung slack and his breath was laboured, obstructed by his lolling tongue. He looked about seventy years old.

Nuri gave Theo a clean white tea towel to use as a bandage and a tight zip-up leather jacket to hold it in place against his waist.

'I can't accept this,' protested Theo. 'It's your jacket.'

'It's not my jacket,' said Nuri sadly. 'It's *his* jacket. And he doesn't wear it anymore.'

Theo zipped the garment on. The ensemble of loud patterned shirt, much-too-small leather jacket, and sodden trousers was not exactly *Barbara Kuhn Show* potential. At least he still had his wallet. He'd intended to transfer it to his suit jacket when he was about to face the crowd at Pages, for the sake of comfort while seated on the hard plastic chair, but had forgotten, and now his suit jacket was no doubt incinerated along with half the books in the store.

'Is your name really Griepenkerl?' asked Nuri as he opened the front door.

'Yes,' said Theo. Fresh air blew into the apartment, rustling old food wrappers and other bits of garbage. A childlike whimper came from behind the couch.

'That's a Jewish name, isn't it?' said Nuri.

Theo shook his head. 'German.'

'I'm glad to hear that,' said Nuri, and, truth be told, he really did look relieved. 'The bus you want is a number 12.'

'Number 12,' said Theo, staggering out into the stairway.

'Make sure you get on that bus,' Nuri called after him. 'This neighbourhood is bad news. People get hurt.'

The People

Theo Griepenkerl walked uncertainly down a street he'd never seen before. The sun was setting and all around him loomed urban grimness of the most aggressive kind. Large rectangles of vacant ground, stripped back to naked gravel after the demolition of whatever had stood there before, were cordoned off with steel mesh and barbed wire. A necklace of multicoloured trash lined the sidewalks. Mysterious metal oblongs, deposited in amongst the cheap rusty cars by construction firms, had been repeatedly defaced with slapdash graffiti, the graceless hieroglyphics of hip-hop. The squat apartment block where Nuri and the white guy lived seemed to be the only functional residential building in the vicinity, and even that was in doubt: almost all its windows were unlit. Framed against the glowering sky, it resembled a giant tombstone.

'Blowjob, mister?'

A black woman with a nylon blond wig and waxy red lipstick was addressing him from behind a telephone booth whose telephone had been ripped out. Theo paused, befuddled. In recent weeks, hundreds of women had approached him, wanting signatures or consolation or simply to be noticed by The Author. For a moment he thought the blowjob in question was something this woman wanted him to bestow on her.

'Fifteen dollars,' she proposed.

Theo looked her up and down. Her toes and the muscles of her feet were bunched and tortured from the strain of keeping a purchase on her ridiculously high-heeled shoes; her legs trembled slightly with the effort. Even her matronly cleavage trembled, the soft dusky flesh quivering like Jell-O. Tattooed on the curve of one breast was a long-tailed bird, caught in flight towards her throat.

Theo fumbled his wallet out of his wet trouser pocket, extracted a twenty dollar bill.

'Keep the change,' he said, and hurried away.

He couldn't actually hurry very fast; it was more an accelerated stumble. If anyone decided to follow him – the prostitute, for example, or a gang of muggers – he would have no chance. Each step sent a jab of pain through his side. He tried limping, in case it helped. It didn't.

Several hundred steps later, he reached the main street. It was a main street like any other, a gallery of consumerist façades obscuring the vestiges of much older architecture. Cars cruised back and forth under a web of electricity wires and traffic gadgetry. The specialist shops had closed for the day, but the convenience stores, takeaway joints and video shops were still open, and people were wandering in and out of them, or just generally hanging around. There was laughter, and negotiation, and spirited dispute about a range of subjects other than *The Fifth Gospel*. Life was going on.

Theo went into a convenience store and bought a bottle of water. He considered buying a pack of cigarettes as well, but his throat still felt scorched from the explosion in the bookshop. Maybe he had discovered the secret of quitting.

Before allowing him to walk away with the water bottle, the checkout guy scrutinised Theo's five dollar bill for what seemed like a full minute. Theo wondered if he'd given the cashier a fifty by mistake. But eventually the bill got stashed in the cash register and Theo was handed his change.

'Thank you,' said Theo.

'Have a good night,' drawled the cashier.

Theo stood on the street outside the store and guzzled water from the bottle. He spilled some on his clothes and looked down to wipe it off. A hunk of the white tea towel was drooping out of the bottom of his leather jacket, revealing a pinkish blush of blood. He tucked it back in, and leaned into the store's doorway.

'Excuse me,' he called to the operator, over the heads of the people queuing up with their purchases. 'How far is the nearest hospital?'

The operator ignored him but an old lady in the queue pointed a gnarled finger due west and said, 'Number 12 bus.'

'Thank you,' said Theo.

He walked further down the street, sucking on the bottle. He wished he was in a warm, clean bed, his skin dry and fragrant, dusted to a silky finish with talcum powder. Maybe he should forget the hospital and check into a hotel instead. Then he could bleed to death in comfort rather than spending half the night waiting in an A&E ward jammed shoulder to shoulder with lowlifes and bums.

He swerved to avoid colliding with a fast-moving couple, and blundered into a trash can. The ground felt uneven underfoot, and the hems of his trouser legs started flapping. He was standing over a ventilation grille that was blowing warm air up from the subway. Bliss. He positioned himself so that the maximum amount of hot breeze penetrated his clothing. If he stood here for a full half hour, his pants would dry out and there would no longer be sodden fabric scratching his hips and thighs as he walked. That would be very nice. Absence of suffering was definitely a noble aim.

He stood above the vent for about eight minutes, enjoying the anticipation of feeling better, until he realised that he was about to black out, and that, if he fell forehead first onto this metal grille, his noble aim of avoiding suffering would be spoiled. So he walked on.

Or tried to. His progress down the street was impeded by a tall black guy wearing a green, yellow and red striped T-shirt with a majestic lion's head printed on it. A Rastafarian, maybe, although he didn't have the Medusa head of dreadlocks. His hair was clipped close to his skull. He was, in fact, the spitting image of John Coltrane. Put him in a natty tailored suit and he'd *be* Coltrane.

'You look lost, brother,' said the Rasta. He didn't sound Jamaican at all, more Bronx. 'Have you heard about Jesus?'

'Yes,' said Theo. 'I've heard about Jesus.'

A big grin. 'You don't *look* it, brother.'

'I'm not feeling too hot,' said Theo. 'Gunshot wound.'

'Hey, I got one of those, too,' said the Rasta, and immediately lifted his shirt. Theo leaned closer to appraise the nasty scar displayed on the left pectoral, near the armpit. The man's physique was otherwise superb.

'Iraq, brother,' he said.

'Iraq?' echoed Theo.

'I'm a marine. Ex-marine.'

'A Rastafarian Christian ex-marine?'

The image of Coltrane allowed his shirt to fall back over his wound. 'I'm movin' away from the Rasta thing,' he said. 'Haile Selassie was a great man, a great, great man, but he ain't the Messiah. There can only be one Messiah.'

'A lot of people feel that way,' agreed Theo. Tiny lights had begun to swim back and forth along his vision, like miniature fish.

'The Rasta thing was, like, a phase after I got back from Iraq,' the Coltrane commando explained. 'I couldn't just come home and fit in with regular folks.'

'I can appreciate that.'

'We doin' some *eee*vil shit over there, you know that?'

'I know that.'

'They told us we're goin' there to save their ass. Don't believe it, man! We don't save nobody's ass. We just bust the place up. And Iraq is the cradle of civilisation, did you know that?'

'Yes, I . . . I've read something to that effect.'

'The Garden of Eden was located there. In Basra.'
The Coltrane guy whacked his brow with his palm,
to indicate a blinding realisation. 'I was patrolling the
Garden of Eden, man, with a grenade hangin' on my
belt, ready to shoot any mo-fo that moved! That ain't
right.'

'No, it isn't.' Theo was shifting his balance from
foot to foot. The wound in his side was burning,
broiling, as though a germ barbeque was being
prepared in there. 'Look, I'd better get going. Can I
give you some money?'

'How much you need, brother?'

'No, can *I* give *you* some money?'

The Coltrane commando smiled broadly. 'You
think I'm some kinda panhandler, brother? I don't
want your money. I want to spread the word of Jesus.'

'I appreciate that.' Theo was thinking of something less lame to add when he experienced a brief
interruption of consciousness. A moment or two, no
more. Just long enough to find himself in the arms
of the marine, being held vaguely upright by rock-
hard muscles. 'I'm sorry, I'm sorry.'

'You better go to a hospital, dude,' said Coltrane. Each syllable was spoken with exaggerated distinctness, as though he doubted Theo's capacity to absorb good advice. 'You promise me that?'

'I promise,' said Theo, staggering onto his own feet again.

'Get your body fixed up, then fill it with Jesus,' said Coltrane. 'Worked for me.'

'Thanks,' said Theo. He was already walking away when he felt something papery being pressed into his hand. He hoped it wasn't Coltrane's hard-earned welfare money.

'Read that, brother,' the voice rang out after him. 'It's the most important document you will ever read. It will change your life. I guarantee it, brother.'

'Thank you, thank you very much.'

Theo tottered onwards. His progress towards the hospital would have to be more straightforward from now on, or he would never get there. He would have to ignore anyone who called out to him. One foot in front of the other, march march march.

A sixth sense warned him to stop in his tracks.

He'd almost collided with a metal pole, planted well into the kerb. The pole was crucifix shaped, with an icon of a bus at the top and a crossbar inscribed with the names of streets and the number 12.

Theo swung into the shelter and sat down on the seat provided. He unzipped his leather jacket slightly, slipped Coltrane's pamphlet inside, and zipped it up again. He got the impression that, inside his jacket, things were wetter and soggier than they ought to have been if his wound was as superficial as Nuri had estimated.

Sitting down did him good. It was an excellent idea; his legs approved. He had walked too long. There was no reason for it anymore. The white guy with the shotgun was not going to catch up with him now, nor would the prostitute seize him by the arm and demand her blowjob. He could relax.

'Excuse me.' A female voice near his ear.

He turned. There was a woman sitting next to him on the bench, a fortyish woman with kindly eyes, a big nose and long dark hair. She was the only other person waiting for the bus.

'I hope I'm not out of line,' she said, 'but haven't I seen you someplace?'

'I don't think so,' he said. 'I'm not from New York.'

'Maybe on TV?'

He hesitated, dredging his mind for a convincing alternative explanation. But he was too tired, too weak to play games.

'Maybe,' he said. 'I . . . I'm an author.'

'Really?' Her respect was unfeigned, requiring minimal extra encouragement to cross the threshold into outright adulation. 'May I ask what books you've written?'

'Just one,' he sighed. 'It's called *The Fifth Gospel*.'

Her eyes narrowed; small creases appeared between her brows as she tried to place the title.

'I don't think . . . I'm sorry, I don't think I've come across it.'

His relief was so profound that he broke into a smile. There must be a God. 'That's OK,' he said.

'My husband and I have a young family,' she explained. 'We don't get as much time to read as we used to.'

'That's OK.'

'Is your book successful? I mean, has it achieved . . . what you were hoping it would achieve?'

Again he smiled. She was smart, this lady. A deft communicator. By not putting a figure on success, by not even mentioning sales, she was doing her bit to preserve his dignity. The way she'd phrased it, even a lousy few hundred copies might qualify as a success, if his hopes for the book had been appropriately modest. Such tact, such grace, from a stranger at a bus stop.

'It's done very well, I guess, considering,' he said. 'I can't complain.'

She nodded, already searching for the safest way to keep the conversation going. 'Who's your publisher?'

'Elysium.'

'Elysium!' Again her respect was unmistakably genuine. 'Wait till I tell Joe! Elysium is the publisher of the most wonderful book, a book that's very precious to us. It's changed our lives!'

He couldn't stop smiling. If he grinned any wider his head was liable to fall off. 'It's good when that happens,' he said.

'Oh, but the story gets even better!' she enthused. 'We ordered our copy second-hand from Amazon. And when we took it out of the wrapper and opened up the first page, it was autographed! Imagine that! Handwritten in ink by Jonas Liffring, right there!'

'Amazing,' he said. He wished the New York City Transit Authority provided pillows in their shelters. He was so incredibly tired.

'We must have read that book a hundred times,' she said.

'What's it called?'

'*Sing Times Seven*,' she said. 'It teaches children, little children, math. Our kids are two and a half and four. And they know their multiplication tables already! It's like a miracle.'

'Wow,' he said.

The number 12 bus pulled up at last, and the woman got to her feet. Theo did too. He was still smiling as he took his first step towards the brightly lit door. Then he fell. Damn it, he fell.

He was out like a light. Try as he might, he couldn't rouse himself, couldn't unwrap the shroud of darkness that had enveloped him, pulling him down into a place where time ceased to matter and centuries could elapse as easily as seconds. For an eternity he lay trapped there, resigned to an eternity more, and another eternity after that. From time to time, dead people came to visit him, speaking not a word, but staring. To each he said, *I'm sorry*. To Marty Salati. To the man burned by gasoline in Santa Fe. To Mr Muhibb in the Mosul museum. To the nameless girl from Kansas. Apparently satisfied, they drifted off again, leaving him in the dark.

But then, suddenly, although he could not yet see, he could feel. Invisible hands were carrying him. Bodiless voices were murmuring concern. He was being rescued. A warm hand was stroking his face, patting it gently.

'Stay with us, stay with us,' a female voice spoke in his ear. She was holding his hand, and he squeezed it.

'That's right,' she said. 'You hold on.' And, as the vehicle thrummed all around them, she began to sing:

'*One times one is one . . .*'

Epilogue: Amen

All this, and more, I saw and heard at the foot of our Saviour's cross. The things I have written down for you are the least of what I understood then; the most glorious understandings elude my ability to write of them. For the hand that holds the pen is attached to the body that aches and growls.

And that is our misfortune, brothers and sisters: we speak of things that cannot be spoken. We seek to store understandings in our gross flesh that gross flesh cannot contain, like a madman who would snatch a moonbeam and put it in his purse. We try our best to tell a story, so that others might be led towards Jesus, but Jesus is not a story. He is the end of all stories.